MARIA MERCURIO

EVERNIGHT PUBLISHING ®

www.evernightpublishing.com

MARIA MERCURIO

DEDICATION

This book is dedicated to my friends and family that have been so wonderfully supportive on my writing journey. Thank you for helping me to realize my dream.

MARIA MERCURIO

MILES AWAY FROM HOME

Survival, 3

Maria Mercurio

Copyright © 2024

This isn't a sweet love story. We don't often get happily ever after. What defines our character is what we do with the crappy hand we are dealt. Who do we become after the dreams are stripped away?

This is a story about survival.

MARIA MERCURIO

Chapter One

Twenty-Five Years Ago

"Miles!" My mother's raspy yell caused me to jump out of my skin. "Miles, get your ass in here," she screeched.

My little brother's eyes went wide at her summons. He gnawed on his thumb and looked to be on the verge of tears. I put my finger over my lips, urging him to be quiet. He nodded mutely. Winking, I mussed up his hair. A quick reassurance was all I had time to offer. Even though I was only three years older than Tate, I felt it was my job to care for him. He was small for four, and no one in our family was kind to a runt. We had two older brothers that made sure to remind him of this fact daily.

I dragged my feet a bit approaching my ma. Figuring out how not to make her angry was a puzzle. As far as alphas were concerned, she was the scariest, Daddy almost seemed cuddly in comparison. She wasn't an overly large woman, my daddy had a good hundred pounds of muscle on her. Her frame could best be described as slightly skeleton-like. She wasn't physically intimidating, but there was a fierceness to her that made even the unsuspecting cringe if she happened to glance at them. Her ability to hold a grudge was legendary—it set her apart from any other alpha I'd ever met. Most alphas led a pack with a sense of obligation for the members. Not my momma. She ruled through fear and intimidation. Once on her bad side, there wasn't a way back. Ever.

Momma was looking out the kitchen window toward the front yard when I reached her. I held my breath rather than announce my presence. She looked pissed. Her fingers drummed out an angry thump on the chipped tile countertops. She was sucking down a cigarette and blowing out smoke like an angry dragon. "Good riddance," she muttered in a barely audible rumble.

Realizing she wasn't speaking to me, I glanced out the window to see what had her riled up. "Where's Tika going?" I asked before I could stop myself. Our pack's omega was stuffing three duffle bags in the back seat of a banana-yellow VW Beetle. She looked up and caught my eye when she shut the door. The smile she gave me was wobbly as she rubbed her watery eyes with the back of a fiercely shaking hand. My heart hurt seeing her sad. A middle-aged woman sat calmly in the driver's seat, elbow hanging out the window, sunglasses askew in her dark-brown hair as she stared without blinking at my mother. I'd seen her before. This was another alpha! An alpha that was taking away the woman that raised me. The only person in this entire pack that watched out for Tate and me.

Without thinking, I started to run to stop her. My mother's wiry arm shot out and her hand clawed into my shoulder. "If the bitch wants to leave us, let her."

"No, Momma, the full moon is only two days away. Who's gonna take care of Tate? We can't leave him alone." I struggled to take a breath. Fear tore at my insides. "Why's she leaving us?" I almost started crying. Omegas didn't leave their packs, not when there were children too young to make the change.

My mother crushed out her cigarette in the sink while her other hand's iron grip kept me from moving an inch. The cloying scent of smoke and heavy perfume made me queasy. My momma rarely touched me except for the occasional scuff on the back of the head. I couldn't remember a time that being close to her didn't result in pain. Tika was the hugger. Tika was the one that blew on your scuffed knees and sang you a lullaby if she found you huddled under blankets unable to brave the night. Things I knew deep down I would never experience again once she left.

An engine revved, followed by the crunch of tires backing up on our gravel driveway. The thought of her leaving without saying goodbye had me seeing red. "What did you do? She wouldn't leave me and Tate like this!" I screamed.

"Watch your mouth, boy. I don't have to explain shit to you." She shook me a bit before letting go. I stumbled back hitting the kitchen table. My hands curled into fists, but I kept my head down and avoided eye contact. It was never wise to take an alpha head on.

"Where's Daddy?" I mumbled swallowing any angry inflections in my tone. Generally, my father wasn't a person I would go to for solving a problem. I tried to lay low and avoid him as much as possible. Yet, if Momma wasn't going to do anything about Tika leaving, he was the only one who might.

"He's off stopping that damn social worker from coming on our property. No thanks to you." Her stormy grey eyes pinned me in place. "Or Tika." The fight went out of me hearing that. I understood what all this was about now.

A few months back Tika started taking Tate with us to our weekly library visits. We were homeschooled, changing into wolves every month made it hard to attend public school. Tika thought it was time to teach Tate to read. I was thrilled he would be coming with us, my baby brother was my best friend. The days when we left him home were always tough on Tate. The other kids in the pack were bigger, older, and bullied him. Most likely they got a rush out of tormenting an alpha's son. Especially since the few times he complained or cried, my mother gave him a proper beating for showing weakness.

Tate was a blanket of bruises on his best day. The crinkly white-haired librarian never said a word to us, but she watched Tate come in each week. A month later a nice lady in a cheap grey suit started showing up. She had skin the color of gingerbread and I swear she smelled like fresh-baked cookies. Her frizzy hair was pulled back into a tight bun with pencils jutting out. She would offer one to Tate when he was practicing making his letters using only his fingers. My little brother was a shy one, but this lady's bright smile had him pulling up a chair and sitting beside her. I should have kept better watch on him. I didn't think this kind woman could or would do us any harm. Last week she cornered Tika:

"I'm his nanny. I've never seen anything bad happen." I heard Tika speaking as I finished putting away my books in the stacks. I turned the corner to see her shaking her head in denial and holding up her hands looking scared.

"He looks malnourished and severely abused." The bun lady folded her arms across her chest. *"I realize this is your employer, but surely the welfare of the child is paramount."*

I wasn't sure exactly what she was saying, but I got the gist that it was about Tate. This lady was worried about him. I looked around and saw he was off playing on the rug with some human kids. The old librarian had put out toys for story time.

"I'm sorry," Tika whispered back. *"I don't have anything to say."* The omega noticed me standing nearby. *"Miles, go get your brother. It's time to go home."*

****

"None of that was Tika's fault!" I protested.

My mother huffed out an aggravated breath. "Sure as shit is. She should have known better. Never trust the humans. Why I expected better from her, I have no idea. She can't even shift. She's not truly one of us. It was useful to have her around to watch those of you too young for the change, but we don't need her reject kind anymore."

"What about Tate? He's only four. It's at least a year before he joins us." I looked down the hallway hoping he couldn't hear.

My mother followed my stare. She pursed her lips in disgust. "Yup, he's going to be a problem we need to get rid of. That's why I called for you."

My stomach soured as if I drank acid. "What … what do you mean?" I stuttered.

"If we leave him here alone when the change happens and the social worker comes sniffing around again, it will be cops to deal with. Pack's big enough. We can afford to lose the runt." She stared back down at me expectantly.

"No. Tate's your son. You can't mean that." I took an involuntary step back.

She angled her head assessing me. "I'd have your brothers take him into the woods, but they'd be cruel. Sending you with him would be a kindness." I stood in complete shock while my mother laid out a plan to get rid of my baby brother. "Pack some food and a sleeping bag. Hike until he can't figure his way home. When you change in two nights, your wolf will know to join up with the pack. After we change back, we'll go back and look for him." She shrugged as if it was no big deal what she asked.

"In the woods! All alone! He could die…" Tears

flooded my cheeks at the thought.

My mother pinched my face, her thumb on my cheekbone, her palm covering my mouth, and her fingernails piercing my other cheek. Effectively silencing any further protests I could utter. She leaned in close, eyes narrowed to slits. "He will have food and shelter. If he's too weak to survive three nights outside during the summer, then he isn't fit for this pack." She loomed over me. I could feel her certainty. She believed this was the right thing to do. The pack bonds sung with conviction. This would protect the pack. She let go of me suddenly and straightened up. "Go on before it gets dark. Find a spot by water. That will make it easier for him."

"I can't." Panic gripped me knowing I wouldn't change her mind.

"Then I'll ask your brother Scott to take him."

Scott was fourteen and the eldest. He was also slightly crazy. Tate was terrified of him. Scott liked to threaten Tate by pinning him down and putting a lighter near his hair. Flicking it on and off, on and off. He only released our brother the last time because poor Tate peed his pants in fear of being burned, and Scott didn't want to get any piss on him.

"I'll do it." I choked out the words, feeling sick.

My mother nodded like it had been a forgone conclusion. "That's my boy."

Chapter Two

Twenty-Five Years Ago

I did exactly what my mother asked me to do, until I couldn't. I did pack up food. I did get sleeping bags, a change of clothes, and a flashlight. I left the house knowing it might be the last time being with Tate. What I couldn't do was take my baby brother deep in the woods and hope he would survive in the wild, alone, at four years old. Instead, I did a thing I never thought to have the courage to do. I stole twenty dollars from my daddy and walked us seven miles to the nearest bus stop. Tate was dragging after mile two, his little legs half the size of mine, but there was no way I would coddle him. We needed to make it to the bus bench before five or my entire plan would be ruined.

I checked my neon-green plastic digital wristwatch for, like, the hundredth time. "Come on now! We're almost there. Bus is coming in twenty." I reached back to take his clammy hand in mine.

"It's so hot, Miles," he whined. "Can't you give me any more water?"

I jerked the pack from my shoulders and pulled out the thermos. The water was lukewarm, but Tate gulped it down like it was a slushy. "That's enough," I grunted. "You're going to get a cramp and walk even slower."

"Where are we going? Where's Tika?" These same questions had been pretty much on repeat for almost two hours.

"I told you, Tika is gone and that means there is no one to take care of you. We have to get you away from the house." I kept walking, but this time Tate didn't follow dutifully behind me. "Dang it, Tate. There is no time for this!"

"I want Tika!" He slumped on the ground refusing to move.

I leaned over and yanked him up with more force than I'd ever used before. His eyes crinkled in fear. He shrank away from me expecting to be hit. It burned me up, but there was only one way to get him on that bus. "Listen to me, runt. Tika left us."

"You're lying! Omegas don't leave packs. They don't stop loving us and walk away!" He sniffled and rubbed his nose across his sleeve.

"Sometimes the truth isn't something you can see clearly," I explained. "Sometimes people have to do things they don't want to do, but that doesn't mean they don't care."

"I want to go home!"

"Look! The change is coming. Momma thought you'd make a better wolf snack than messing things up at home while we're away. She told me to get you good and lost. I was feeling bad about it all, but if you're gonna be a big baby, maybe I should leave you."

"I'm not a baby," he seethed glaring at me.

Tate's angry eyes made me feel awful low, but my words got him to stand. "Well, come on then. See that bench there?" I pointed. "That's where the bus comes. You can rest till it shows up."

Tate walked behind me, arms folded over his chest, silent tears streaking down his face. I ignored it all and hoped I read the bus schedule right. My older brothers and I took the bus once a week during the summer to work on a communal farm run by a shifter council. The work wasn't too hard, we mainly picked berries. They fed us well and we got to take food back to our pack. I liked it mainly for the bus ride. We would stop and pick up kids along the way from other packs, and I could see how others of our kind lived.

One particular pack always drew my attention. The children from that pack never needed to work on the communal farm. That pack was rich and had massive farmlands of their own. The bus always went by their lands and my older brothers would grumble about what a waste that Reds owned it. That was where I was taking Tate now.

I was relieved when I saw the bus approach from the right direction in the distance. We made it! I put my hand on Tate's shoulder to congratulate him, but he moved away from my touch. His lips were pressed into a tight line and he wouldn't look at me. I stopped myself before I leaned in to smooth things over. It was better this way. Better to be angry than sad.

Four-year-old curiosity got the better of Tate once we made it on the bus and sat down. The hum of the air-conditioning cooled his temper along with our sweat-soaked bodies. "Where are we going, Miles?"

My daddy always said our mother was relentless. I asked him what it meant. He told me it's when you never give up. Little Tate might have a bit more of Momma in him than anyone thought. "You'll see when we get there."

"Like a surprise?" Tate perked up. "Like a party?"

I scoffed at that. "No, silly. Why would we go to a party?"

He shrugged and bounced repeatedly in his seat. The cool air and the promise of a surprise restored his energy. Pointing out the window every few minutes he repeated a single question over and over. "What's that?"

I just started making up silly stuff after answering the first ten times. "That's a dragon. That's an alien. That's a flying monkey."

Tate giggled as he pointed at a tree and called it a "talking rainbow." It was nice to hear him laugh. He usually stayed quiet in the house, best to not be seen or heard. The drive flew by as we both cracked each other up making believe the plain world outside was filled with craziest things we could dream up.

"Now *that*,"—I jerked my head as I grabbed our things—"is our stop."

Tate left the bus in a totally different mood from when he got on. The bus driver winked at us as we waved and hopped out. The summer heat smacked us in the face as soon as we stepped on the asphalt. Both our shoulders slumped as the humid air settled on us, making the burden of walking ten times heavier.

"I don't want to walk anymore," Tate gave me puppy eyes. "My feet hurt."

"I know, bud." I ruffled his hair. "I'm not keen on walking either. We just need to get to the end of this road."

Tate squinted down the street trying to see the end of it. "How far?"

"Not sure. Never been," I confessed.

Tate's bottom lip trembled. "Why here, then?"

"Here is a new home. That's the surprise. A better home," I stated with more conviction than I felt.

"A new home?" A note of wonder accompanied his high-pitched voice.

I nodded and trotted on, afraid he would ask questions I would never be able to answer. Worried I wasn't doing the right thing. This pack always looked so clean and nice. The kids were close and stuck together like a pack should. Did that mean they would treat Tate the same? Maybe this life would be even worse for him? I shook my head praying the thoughts would jump out and leave me be. This pack had to be better, better than dying in the woods alone at least.

Daddy constantly grumbled about the Reds, saying they were a bunch of bleeding hearts. Momma said they shouldn't even call themselves wolves and probably were vegetarians. To her, Reds were not tough enough to hurt anything. I was counting on that. Counting on them taking one look at chubby cute little Tate and knowing he was worth keeping. Even if Tate did survive alone in the woods during this change, there would always be the next month and the month after that. This had to be for the best.

The smell of roasting meat and woodsmoke made my stomach rumble. Guess they weren't vegetarians after all. For Tate's sake, I hoped the other stuff was true. We were getting close to the gate signaling the border for the community. My feet started to drag. This was it for Tate and me. I'd be leaving him. We wouldn't be pack. He's too little to feel the bonds yet. They don't come till a Wa'ya's first change. Next year when Tate had his first shift, he would bond to the pack he's with.

The thought stopped me cold.

Tate looked at me, head tilted. "Why you stopping now? All day it was go, go, go."

I swallowed, even though my mouth felt as dry as a cracked rubber tire. "I'm not going any further with you. You need to go the rest of the way on your own. An alpha named Austin lives in the big house. You tell him our pack doesn't want you no more. He'll let you come in."

"What?" Fear made Tate's voice quiver. "You said a new home."

"Yes, a new home for you. Not me." I had a long haul still, just one more day till the change. I would camp for the night and take the bus back in the morning. Then hike into the woods, where we were already supposed to be, set up camp to look like I did take Tate with me, and wait till my wolf came.

"You don't want to be my brother?" The dust from the road coated his sweaty face, but it was the lines of fat tears that punched me in the gut.

"I can't be. Momma said to get rid of you." I had to hold my breath to stop myself from crying in front of him.

"Momma doesn't like me 'cause I'm small," Tate said miserably.

"You ain't always gonna be small."

Tate gazed up the road. "Maybe they won't like me 'cause I'm small."

I sniffed and rubbed my nose against my shoulder. "They seem nice."

He looked at me sharply. "Then stay!"

"The change is only two nights away. I'd be a strange wolf here. They might rip me up. You ain't pack yet. I told you, Momma said to get rid of you. So," I extended my arm up the road. "Go on and get."

"You gonna come back after?" Tate kicked at the rocks on the dirt road.

I gritted my teeth, holding back from giving him a hug. It would be better if he wanted to leave. Tate wouldn't bond with a new pack if he thought I was going to come for him. "Nope." I repositioned the pack on my shoulders. "Maybe I'll see you around in a few, but don't go looking for me to rescue you."

Ugly loud sobs escaped from Tate and he huddled over grabbing his stomach as if kicked. I took three large steps away from him. It was too late to do anything about this now. There was no Tika to care for him and our momma felt the pack was big enough. This was the best thing I could do for him. I picked up a rock from the road and clipped him in the arm with it. He looked up with a mixture of shock and hurt.

"Go on now. Head down that road." I was firm, imagining my daddy barking orders.

"Miles?" Tate took a step toward me, disbelief marking his features.

"You heard me, runt!" Spittle flew from my lips as I leered. "We are done with you. We don't need a runt in the pack." I turned on my heel and walked away. At first I could hear him still taking steps toward me, but when I didn't look back, he stopped. I had a moment of happiness when his footfalls sped up and he ran away from me, up the road to where the red wolf pack lived. They would accept him. They would see how gentle and kind he was. They just had to.

Chapter Three

Present Day

"I can't believe you made me leave her like that! The kidnapping was bad enough, but to leave her on the side of the road with an obvious concussion. Raff is going to be out for blood." Akela stomped on the dashboard with her foot.

Her outburst was actually a relief. She hadn't spoken a word as I drove for the last forty minutes. Besides the sound of her grating teeth, she was the picture of silence. Staring pointedly out the window, she avoided any interaction with me. I turned to her and smiled, excited she decided to engage me in any way.

"What the hell are you smiling at? Are you completely deranged and broken?" Using her index finger, she made a circle gesture in front of her face. "In case you're confused. This is me. Being angry. At you!"

"I guess." I shrugged.

"What do you mean, you guess?" She threw up her hands as her voice rose an octave. "I'm literally telling you I'm mad."

"I guess I'm broken," I clarified.

Her rage deflated and she slumped back into the chair. Taking a slow breath in and out, she scrubbed her hands over her face. Long golden strands covered eyes the color of the Caribbean Sea. Not that I've ever been, but there are these brochures hanging at the travel agency next door to the garage where I work. I pass them on my way to grab lunch every day. The water always made me think of Akela, so alluring, you just wanted to dive right in.

"Oh, Miles," her voice caught and my gut clenched at the sound. "What are we going to do?"

I liked that she said *we*. Maybe it was finally dawning on her there was only one path forward for us. "What do you mean?"

Those piercing eyes searched my face for answers I knew she wouldn't find. "It's like we're that damn U2 song."

She meant *With Or Without You*. The irony that it played the one and only time I danced with her wasn't lost on me. "You have to live with me. We tried the other way longer than what is natural for our kind." I didn't mean to sound gruff, but I'd waited years for her. She may not have been the one that broke me, but she was responsible for me acting deranged. I know I didn't deserve her. Akela was this perfectly beautiful untouchable thing. I was a giant hulking mess. She was my fated mate, and unfortunately for her, it meant I was also her fate.

A combination of a sob and a strained laugh passed her lips. "Where are we going, by the way?"

Abducting Raff's woman hadn't been a thing I planned out well. Don't get me wrong, I very much wanted to do it, had fantasized about how to get even with that arrogant prick Raff, but most of the success was dumb luck. Caius, my "no self-control" pack mate, and I were driving to get parts for a car we were fixing up. I saw Chloe and her pack driving on the freeway and told Caius to follow. We did it for hours without any idea if it would work. I worried they would not take the chance and ever leave Chloe alone. Then opportunity knocked when she ditched their omega and headed off on her own. It was then my convoluted plan of forcing the issue with Akela unfolded. Pulling one over the golden boy alpha was icing on the cake.

"We have a cabin we use for the full moon, but I need to make a stop at my house first. I don't have provisions with me." I could feel her scrutiny as a slow warmth settled on my cheeks. I shifted in my seat.

"Looks like we are driving in the direction of *my* home."

She was totally going to bust my balls for this. "My house is nearby."

She made a quick little humming sound. "How close by?"

My daddy always told me only lie to your mate for a damn good reason. Of course, my momma was scary as shit, so he found lying to her necessary often enough to save his sorry ass. I wasn't sure which way to play this with Akela. It would have been better just to head to the cabin and meet up with the guys. I just hadn't thought it through. "I live off of Pleasant Hill Road."

I could hear her intake of breath. "That's Austin pack territory. How can your wolf stand it? How has this never been an issue?"

"Well, I don't stick around for the shift. I'm in my own territory for that week." I couldn't resist glancing her way. Hoping she would let it go, but knowing she would wring the entire embarrassing truth out of me.

Her feet dropped from the dashboard and she leaned forward with pursed lips. "Are you telling me your pack stays only a couple of miles away from mine? And every month you drive what must be at least a hundred miles away?"

"I live alone. The guys are spread out. Only Kyle, our omega, stays at the cabin. It's quiet and peaceful there but can get boring fast. We all meet up when it's time."

"Why would you do that?" she asked incredulous. "It doesn't sound like much of a pack if you can only stand each other one week a month."

The back of my neck felt like a hot water bottle leaked on it. I was a hundred degrees and sweaty. "You're going to make me say it, aren't you?"

Akela's manicured hands flew up. "Say what?" She acted mystified, but I wasn't buying it.

"It's too difficult to be farther from you. I get jittery if I'm too far away," I mumbled.

"But what about your pack?" she continued to press.

"You know it doesn't work without you. We just have our pledge to each other, but we're not a pack until you decide to make us so," I gritted out the words.

"Raff's guys bunked together. They worked together and traveled around together," was her snide reply. The little know-it-all apparently knew next to nothing.

I jerked the car to the side. My pulse sped up as I turned to face her. "Raff didn't know who his fated mate was for over a decade though, did he?"

She backed up, those ocean-blue eyes widening at my tone.

"I've known, even though you have pretended that this thing was never real. You know it isn't possible for me to stay away. So, yes! I live only a few fucking miles from your house, because you refused to acknowledge me! Yes, my pack is scattered! Because no one else wants to live this close to another big pack. It makes them edgy. But I had to! This was the only way to be near you. Had you ever once agreed to come to my home in all these years, this would not be such a damn surprise!"

My ragged breathing filled the car for several heartbeats. Those hypnotizing eyes of hers softened slightly. Her tongue moistened her pouty pink lips and my thoughts went haywire. I knew it wasn't an invitation to taste her, yet it was all I could think of. My anger simply forgotten. This was her power she pretended not to be aware of. I was nothing but a puppet to her whims.

Delicate fingers reached up and stroked the side of my face soothingly. Her exhale, more of a sigh, was warm against my skin. I stopped breathing entirely. No one in my entire life had ever touched me so softly. When she dropped her hand, I felt its loss. "You are a complete paradox, Miles. I am utterly confused by you."

Her befuddled expression caused me to smile. "Maybe if you stuck around long enough that wouldn't be the case."

Disgust ghosted her features. I expected it, but it still hurt to see scorn replace the moment of tenderness. "You are Machiavellian. Might makes right. Forcing me to shift with your pack or you hurt my friend. Take what you want and screw the rest. Don't try to con me into thinking there are layers."

I groaned as I put the car back into "drive." I'd hoped this wouldn't be yet another battle between us. My eyes skimmed over the little bag she brought with her and a pang of guilt sprung up at my actions. For a spilt-second, I considered asking if she needed anything from her house, but I couldn't risk it. In Austin's eyes, I was scum. Even if he knew she was my mate, there was a chance he would try to stop me from leaving with Akela. I was thirty-two years old and an alpha in my own right. I waited thirteen years for this woman to see me as her mate. I sure as shit wasn't going to allow anyone to get in the way of that anymore, not Austin's pack or Raff or his mate. Hell, not even Akela was going to stand in the way of the reality of the situation. There were only a few days before the change would happen and we were all going to be a pack when it was over. I would make sure of it.

Chapter Four

Twenty-One Years Ago

Unlike human kids, I looked forward to the end of summer every year. Other kids would complain about going back to school, but when you grew up in a pack, homeschooling was year-round. Either classwork or manual work every day were my only options. The last week of summer was the only real break we ever got. The packs would choose a different spot each year and we would come together in a big camping cookout.

Despite pack animosity, hundred-year-old feuds, and regional differences, the summer campout was always well attended. Almost thirty years before I was born, the Wa'ya started having issues. Less and less females were born, and out of those that were, fewer and fewer could make the change. Before, finding a mate and having a family meant not having to venture far. For the young men now, especially the alphas, this week was the only time they could find a mate. To keep us from going extinct, one week a year the Wa'ya tolerated each other. Sure, there were plenty of ways to still be nasty to the other packs, but that stuff was done quietly. Being evicted from the end-of-summer gathering could be a death warrant for a pack. Even my momma played nice. It was also the only time in the entire year I could see my little brother.

Tate just had a birthday in early August, he turned eight. I'd saved up enough money to buy him these trading cards called Pokémon. I didn't understand how to play with them, and Dad would never let us watch the show when it was on saying the voices were too annoying, but I thought it would be something Tate would love. I overheard him talking to a kid last year about Japanese animation and how cool it was. It was something he watched with his new family. Alpha Austin had placed Tate permanently in his own sister's home. Tate had a sister now and two young twin baby brothers.

I played off dropping him in the woods and meeting up with the pack to not rouse my momma's suspicion. To her credit, she did go and look for him once we changed back. Had she shown any signs of grief, I might have come clean. Three days of searching the woods and both my parents just gave up. We no longer had an omega. It would be a burden to have a child too young to shift. I should have cried and screamed at them more when they stopped looking, made it look more believable that I also thought he was gone. When they saw Tate at the all-pack campgrounds the next year, my momma pinned me with a stare to peel the flesh from my bones.

I held my breath, wondering if she was going to storm over to Alpha Valentina and rip Tate from her hand. I think Valentina wondered the same thing. She looked to be holding onto both Tate and her oldest son Raff in a death grip. Tate was staring at me with his big brown doe eyes. I did what I had to do to protect myself from Momma.

"I guess they found the trash you left out, Momma," I said, hoping she would see I was on her side, and praying Tate didn't hear.

My momma answered with a dry, ugly chuckle. I may not have been found innocent, but showing my meanness won me her forgiveness. She ruffled my hair and turned and walked away. She still doesn't ever make eye contact with Tate. Looks over his head if he's anywhere nearby. Her actions were easy to read, even for a kid. Tate was dead to her.

I was hoping enough years had passed, that

Momma wouldn't watch my every move, and I could try to be Tate's brother again. The birthday gift was my hope at a new start. I was so excited when we reached the campsite. I imagined handing over the gift and we could be brothers again in secret. I missed my best friend.

Dad had a pop-up camper that he hitched behind our Ford pickup. Me and my brothers would stay outside in sleeping bags at night, but we got to ride in the camper during the two-day journey here. It was softer to sit in than the truck bed, less muggy too. Pop was terrible at driving it, though. "Reverse" was his enemy.

After dad's fourth attempt at parking, I hopped out while he cursed up a storm having just torn off part of a tree. Using the distraction, I slipped away to scout out where the other packs set up.

I heard Tate before I saw him. He laughed rarely, being a generally shy kid, but it was distinctive. The sound was a mixture of snorts and cackles. It was hard not to smile listening to it. I checked my back pocket and the box of trading cards was there. This might be my only time to catch him, so I wasn't going to squander it.

At eleven, I was already five foot ten. Tate was still much smaller than me, but compared to the tubby toddlers that were squealing and running around a tree, he had grown quite a bit. I walked close by and whistled a tune we used to both love. Tate's warm chocolate eyes searched me out instantly and a weary frown decorated his face. I made sure no one was looking and huddled up near a large tree that offered the best coverage. Tate stood still staring while the toddler boys attempted to climb on his legs.

"Hey," his voice was pitched lower as he looked around anxiously. "What are you doing here?"

"Dad's having a heck of a time parking the trailer, so I slipped away. I wanted to talk to you." I looked down at the toddlers. "Those the twins you live with?" I asked.

Tate smiled at them fondly. "They act like they're hopped up on sugar all the time, even though Mom is pretty strict with sweets."

Something ugly and oily slithered in my stomach. "Mom?"

Tate rubbed the back of his neck and looked at me slightly defiant. "She told me when I was ready to stop calling her Aunt Marta, I could call her Mom."

"But she's not your momma."

"Really?" Tate challenged. "Marta feels more like my mom than Momma ever did. She wants me, for starters."

I should've let him have this. I wasn't sure why it bothered me to see him happy. Except if they were his family now, what did that make me? "They aren't Greys, though. Those Reds only want you because they know you are better than them."

Tate snorted and looked at me closely with something that felt like pity. "There was a time you might have fit in better with Austin's pack too. You liked to read and discover new things. Austin is a scientist."

The truth was, I hadn't been to the library since our omega left our pack. I'd been reading the same five books for the last four years. We had one computer for all of us to share, and only because Momma had to send in reports of our homeschooling. I usually didn't get a turn on it till after midnight and there was never free time to read for pleasure.

"Sounds lame and nerdy," I couldn't help being a bit defensive.

Tate's face crumpled and he took a step away from me. "Seems like you're fitting in better with your pack these days, though." I instantly felt bad and reached for my back pocket to offer him his gift and say sorry. A flurry of blonde curls and neon pink stopped me. The girl barreled in-between Tate and me. She looked to be close in age to my brother, and I imagined this must be the sister of the twins. Eyes so blue they probably had a crayon color named after them, took in Tate's expression. She reached for Tate's hand, and he quickly clasped hers. I was surprised to see his easy acceptance of public affection. It wasn't a thing our family did.

The girl offered me a ferocious glare, but she was seriously too cute to pull it off. "What do you want, Lurch?" I huffed out a breath, but was unable to answer as she poked me hard in the chest with her free hand. "I think you should go back to where you came from."

"It's okay, Akela." Tate tried to calm her.

She puckered her rose-petal lips. "No, sir, I don't think it is. I can tell he was being mean. I was watching."

"Listen, Akela, is it? Tate is my brother and we were just talking." I tried again to reach for his gift hoping I could patch this all up, when the girl launched herself at me.

Her little hands grabbed at my shirt to pull me down while she rose on her tiptoes attempting to get to my eye level. I would have laughed if I wasn't so shocked.

"Listen here. This is *my* brother. He's not yours anymore! You had your chance to have the absolute best brother in the entire world and you threw it away. I heard about his older brothers, using Tate like a punching bag in the gym. Ain't gonna happen, punk!"

"Akela, stop." Tate tried to pull her off me. She held on for a moment longer, giving me the death glare. Then she stepped away and wiped her hands on her jean shorts. She made a show of it, like I was an infection.

"Listen here, pip-squeak. You don't know

anything about me. Why don't you go play with some dolls?"

"I know enough," she said while crossing her arms over her chest. "I know Tate is better off without you."

"Akela!" Tate looked pained at her words but didn't tell her to take a hike. Maybe the little blonde savage was right. Compared to his new family, the only thing I had to offer was bad memories.

I held up my hands in mock surrender. "Fine by me," I sneered. I walked away, not once looking back, and Tate never called out for me to stop.

That night we had a campfire. The wood was slightly damp and the fire kept nearly going out. The paper we had nearby was burned up. I pulled out the pack of cards and fed them one at a time into the fire.

"What are those?" Dad asked.

I held up a card before flicking it to land on the logs. "These were Tate's."

"Nice," Momma said and laughed. "Not even a full day and you're already swiping stuff from those dumbass Reds and destroying the evidence."

I didn't correct Momma. Praise was hard to come by. I was even awarded an extra marshmallow in front of my older brothers. It took a while for the fire to singe the card and finally catch flame. I told myself once I burned up the entire deck, I would stop thinking about him. But the image of that angelic hellion holding his hand and claiming he was the best brother in the world, played over and over in my head, even after we doused the fire and I crawled into my sleeping bag.

Chapter Five

Present Day

I didn't stay at my place long. Grabbed a cooler, few cases of beer, box of frozen steaks, and a duffle bag of clothes. Everything had been made ready for the week away before I left for the unscheduled abduction. Akela silently appraised my Spartan abode as I ran back and forth to the car. I didn't feel self-conscious. This house was just a place to store my things so I could be near her, so I could see her, so I could be there when she was ready to accept me. Except that day had never come. When I became an alpha and broke away from my parents' pack, I thought I'd become a lone wolf. Life had other plans, though. I picked up loners and stragglers like an old lady with stray cats.

The thing I was most worried about showing Akela was my pack. If she rejected them the same way she constantly rejected me, then that would be it. I needed to make her truly see them, to see *me*. Yet, I hadn't a clue how.

At first, I'd played the role of jerk to keep my brother from trying to return. Then as a teen, it was survival of the fittest. I did what I needed to, things I wasn't proud of. As a man, I sensed the alpha in me. I could no longer stomach having to do as others expected or wanted. By then, though, I'd made quite the reputation as my mom's true son. None of my big scary brothers became alphas. That left Mom with me as sole pack heir.

My mother expected me to return and claim my place as the alpha one day. We'd only spoken twice since I left my former pack, both times she seemed to think I was waiting to find a mate before I returned. I never told her about Akela. No way. I wouldn't go back. Nothing I loved was there.

The errant thought of love had my eyes trailing up long toned legs, hardly hidden by the thin fabric of her leggings. Under the tights, I could see firm muscle definition. Luckily for me, I could continue unobserved with my perusal, as Akela was bent over, scrounging in my fridge. She might be a Tennessee girl, but that ass was all Georgia peach. Alas, womanly intuition was one hundred percent a thing. Her head swiveled back. I was caught ogling. One side of her mouth quirked up, in what I swear was the most adorable evil smile created.

"You got hardly anything edible in here," she complained.

I had to clear my throat twice. "That isn't what I was thinking. Quite the opposite." I stood at my full height forcing her to crane her neck. "I think the sweetest, juiciest thing I have ever seen is in this kitchen."

I wanted to get her to blush, or at least smile. True to form, my Akela rolled her eyes. She never fell for any of my lines. "Is starving me your big plan to win me over?"

I leaned in close and noticed with delight the pulse jumping in her neck. She was more affected than she let on. I reached up, as if to touch her but closed the fridge instead. She released a shaky breath. I chewed on my bottom lip and savored this small victory. "I'm planning on stopping at Bojangles. I was going to use biscuits as part of the grand master plan to make you fall head over heels."

She angled her head appearing to mull it over. "I guess it isn't the worst place to start."

I watched her shimmy out the door in those skintight leggings and had to give it to the woman. She was taking this hostage exchange pretty well. Angry as a cat in the rain at first, but calm as a cucumber now. I quickly squashed down my hopes. This wasn't the first time I thought she'd stay with me. Maybe she'd never agree to truly love me, but at least acknowledge our connection. Each time I swear I had her, she up and walked away. Fool that I was, I let her. All that "if you love something set them free" crap was bullshit. This time I had to make her stay long enough that she couldn't ever be free of me. She was a drug for me, but I needed her to be just as addicted.

****

Akela didn't last long after her belly was full. I watched her head droop to the side with something close to satisfaction. She was comfortable enough to fall asleep beside me. That was a good sign. I needed to focus on the good things. The hour and a half drive should have been tedious. The roads were more congested than usual. I was afraid to turn on the stereo and wake her, so I drove in silence. A plastic bag managed to get stuck in my wheel well making an irritating noise every thirty seconds. About every five minutes I considered pulling over to tear it out. Despite those things, I was unusually content. My mate was with me.

The nerves didn't truly kick in till my tires left the paved highway and started crunching on the gravel. Akela shifted in her seat, slowly starting to wake. Reality set in. She would be meeting my pack for the first time. Over the years one or two might have been nearby, but I had never introduced them as pack. She'd glimpsed Caius at the exchange with Chloe. He was the stoic type, not saying much yet managing to be menacing. Not the best first impression. I never gave a damn about how others perceived my pack mates. These guys were the family I chose. To hell with anyone else's concept on what made a good pack. Akela was the only exception.

Her opinion meant more than mine. A male alpha could pull a pack together, but it took a female alpha to bring the bonds to life.

The dirt road to the cabin started out smooth, but changed to massive potholes and rain-made ridges about a mile in. My little Viking goddess jerked awake with a shout as her hand flew to the ceiling to steady her body.

"What the hell," she muttered as she looked around trying to orient herself. "Wow, I crashed hard. I take it we're almost there?"

"Yeah, we got about another two miles of this before we reach the cabin."

"How did you find this place? Really tucked away." She absentmindedly chewed her lip making me want to pull over and kiss her till we ran out of air.

"It belonged to the Norvill pack. This was their territory."

"Was?" Her brows furrowed like when she was pissed at me. "What did you do?"

Kick in the gut fully delivered. "Not anything you're imagining," I grumbled before taking a needed deep breath. "Tom Norvill's wife died about five years ago. His pack hasn't had a female that could shift, let alone an alpha female since then. Pack bonds dissolved. The few guys he had left, joined other packs. Tom, being an alpha, didn't have that choice. He went lone wolf. I met him about two years after her death. He had a lemon of a truck and was getting fleeced by his mechanic. Caius and I worked on it for him. He was a shell of his former self. I remembered how he was at the summer socials— big laugh, large appetite, and a great storyteller."

Akela smiled fondly. "I remember him scaring the crap out of me every summer with his stories. I had to sleep with a light on in my tent."

I nodded having similar memories. "So, when I

saw him thin and sad, I couldn't bring myself to charge him for our services. He gave me this cabin instead."

Her slight frown told me she wasn't buying it. "Just like that? He gave you his family home as payment for working on his car?"

"No," I white-knuckled the steering wheel. She always made me say more than I wanted to. "He hung around the garage the few days it took to work on the truck. He got drinks with Caius and me the first night, and the next day my pack mate Luke invited Tom over for dinner. He didn't realize I had a pack until then. He asked where we went for the change. I told him it depended on the time of year and what we could find away from humans and other packs. Then he handed me the keys. Told me it was too painful a place for him and that he liked thinking about a new pack using it." I shrugged.

"But to keep, like, forever? Maybe it was only supposed to be a loner. Have you seen him since?" she persisted, as usual.

"Yes." I ground my teeth. "He still hasn't ditched that lemon, and I still fix it for him each time."

"What makes you think he won't ask for it back?" she questioned.

"You."

"Me?" Her eyebrows crunch low. "What has any of this got to do with me?"

"When he handed me the keys he said…" I paused knowing I was opening another can of worms. "'You can't expect that mate of yours to live like a bunch of roaming bachelors. Akela comes from a proper home and you need to give her a confirmed territory. You want a real pack, you need to deliver a real pack home.'"

"You talked to him about me?" her voice went soft.

Damn it! I wanted to lie, but lying to one's true mate was a sure path to rejection. This woman would never be satisfied till she humbled me. "I asked him for advice," I mumbled hoping she might not hear.

The delighted smile blooming on her face confirmed she did, in fact, hear. "You asked Tom for relationship advice?"

"Yes," my answer was short and clipped. Her booming laughter caused the tops of my ears to burn. "Glad you find the years of torment you put me through amusing."

"Oh please!" she huffed and crossed her arms over her chest. "You have the emotional capacity of a rock. I'm nothing more to you than a puzzle piece you're obligated to jam in. I'm necessary."

"Of course you're necessary!" My temper spiked. "My body tells me constantly I need you more than I need air."

"Exactly! It's just our biology. It's not love." Her bitter statement was like a hand squeezing around my heart.

The cabin lights were visible in front of us. I pulled into the driveway and put the car in "park," taking a moment before I got out. "I know you believe I'm not capable of love or maybe not even worth you trying to love me," I spoke, my voice catching at the end. She stilled at my words, blues eyes wide and lips firmly clenched. "The guys in there probably won't impress you like your birth pack either. I just want to know if you will give this even the smallest chance? They deserve it. Is this just another blow-off?"

She reached in the back seat and snagged her duffle bag. Her expression somber. "You gave me an ultimatum six months ago. I know what your terms are."

"And?" I prompted.

"I'm here, aren't I?" She opened the door and stood up while I blew out the breath I was holding. Not quite the answer I was hoping. For now, it would have to do. Akela was never one to go easy on me.

Chapter Six

Thirteen Years Ago

Momma alternated between chewing on a hangnail and taking long drags of her cigarette. Her eyes stayed pinned on me, though. An unsettling mixture of pride and cold calculation were her dominant expressions. It would usually have been difficult to look away from her singular focus, my mother's presence was incredibly dominant, but guilt made me only register her on a small scale. My attention was glued to the figure on the bed. My father's comatose body was pale. The sheets were stained red with his blood. His face was a myriad of bruises. I'd come extremely close to killing him.

At six feet seven inches, I wasn't the tallest member of the pack, but I was the strongest. Momma had to have known my alpha tendencies, newly awakened, would challenge my father in wolf form one of these months. Yet neither of my folks had said I should leave. It's a miracle we're both alive after the last change. I only had flashes of anger, growls, and teeth tearing flesh as a memento from last night. My father will heal, but he will also carry the scars of our battle for the remainder of his life. The time frame of that greatly depending on when I planned to leave.

The guilt didn't spring from my wolf side hurting my father. We grew up understanding our other halves weren't evil. Their intentions are instinctual. It's our human side we need to fear. I knew I was taking a risk staying with the pack. For so many years, I'd wanted nothing more than to leave and venture on my own. The sense of pack hadn't been the reason I'd stayed. No. Deep down, I'd wanted to challenge my father. I wanted to see if the man who allowed his younger sons to be bullied and beaten, would have what it took to take me on and win. Turns out, he was as shit of an alpha as a father.

A few months back, I turned nineteen. You don't wake up one day and declare yourself an alpha. It's a feeling that grows. Agitation builds when others make eye contact. This overwhelming urge consumes you to challenge any conversation, even the ones you agree with. Every space you find yourself in feels small and cramped, so you snap at any and every one nearby. In short, young alpha males are total dicks.

Momma knew what was happening to me. She would chuckle off my aggression and smugly tell me in a year or two I'd be able to control the rage. Unfortunately for my father, my wolf hadn't waited. Luckily for my father, he would live, but only if I left. Next change, my wolf would take him out and stake a full claim. It was the way of pack life. "Why didn't you kick me out? You can't get any satisfaction seeing your mate broken and bleeding," I grumbled.

Momma spit the nail she tore from her thumb onto the floor. "I wanted to see what you could do."

"And if it meant killing Dad?" I barked my question at her.

The eerie calculation was back in her eyes. She leaned forward from the chair and rested her elbows on the bed looking at her husband. "He's not my true mate." She shrugged.

"God, what are you saying? You wanted me to kill him?" I looked at her horrified of what she would say next.

"No, I didn't want you to kill him, Miles," she answered exasperated. "Your dad was a hellion as a teen. I did fancy him, but my alpha nature was stronger. My true mate might have balanced me, kept me in check. As a young girl, I didn't much like the idea. I wanted to be *the* alpha of a pack. Twenty-five years later, I find myself slightly bored. He didn't even blink when I suggested we should let you stay as long as you wanted. What alpha male doesn't defend his territory? I wanted to see if you were stronger than him. Make sure I raised you to be an alpha like me."

The words slithered inside. A layer of slime coated me with her distorted praise. "I don't understand what you're saying to me."

She rolled her eyes and groaned. "Go out into the world, son. Find yourself a mate if you can. I'll keep this pack together. When you're ready to come back and claim it proper, you'll make me a proud momma. I can leave a legacy of a strong pack held by a strong alpha, or in the case a mate cannot be found by the time you are ready to return, I can hold the bonds steady for you as long as needed."

Her words sickened me. Claiming the pack meant she did expect me to one day kill my father. It was unlikely the son of a bitch would leave willingly, even after this beating. In a strange way it all made sense, though. My mother always had more control of the pack and our family. She didn't love her husband. If she had, it might have softened her some. Who knew if she was even capable of love?

"I'll go get my things," I muttered.

"No hurry," she said and shrugged. "You got weeks before the next change."

I looked at my dad struggling to breathe through a broken nose. "No, it's time," my voice turned cold. "Best if I'm not here when he wakes up."

My mother's eyes lit up. "I imagine you know best." She nodded. "Pack will be here for you when you're ready to take it."

It would be a cold day in hell before that ever happened. I wasn't in the mood to discuss it, though. My insides were chaffing to get out of this sick room and far away from this place. There were no goodbyes or hugs from my family. My brothers had stayed clear of me once I presented as alpha, my father was unconscious, and I couldn't remember ever having my momma show an ounce of affection. I strode to my room, stuffed clothes in a duffle bag, and made a few trips to the garage for camping gear. After loading up the truck, I drove off not looking back once.

A few miles down the road, something brittle shattered in my chest. This overwhelming sense of loss hit me like a ton of bricks. My bond with the pack was broken. Even though my relationships with my family had been rough, I still had a few friends. I couldn't reach them anymore. The sense of being part of a larger whole had vanished. I should have been grateful to completely distance myself, yet as fucked up as my parents were, the pack animal inside of me didn't like feeling isolated. The loneliness ate at me the further I drove away. It was a chasm I longed to fill back up. Without much more thought, I drove straight to Tate's home.

Tate was sixteen now and almost as big as me. No one in the outside world would expect he was still a kid. I planned to ask him to hit the road with me. We could make a new start, be a family again. Who knows, he might be bored with the quiet life the Reds lived. Maybe he was dying to leave but had no one to go with. The more miles my tires ate up the firmer my certainty became. I was heading in the right direction. The future would be brighter than my past. I wasn't the evil jerk my mother had hoped for. I wasn't a killer.

That didn't mean I was going to drive right up and announce myself. A lone alpha never entered another's pack territory without permission. I highly doubted Mr. High and Mighty Alpha Austin would be rolling out the welcome wagon. I parked a few hundred yards away from their community's main entrance. The gate could keep out my truck, but it would be easy enough to walk to Tate's house.

I waited till dusk when the sun wouldn't expose all movement. I wanted to see if I could catch Tate outside, he used to wait till the last rays of light went away before begrudgingly going home. Not sure if that habit still stuck. Was it his love of nature that kept him outdoors when we lived together or his fear of our mother? I was counting on the sun setting early before dinnertime and most pack kids being out. I knew if it came to breaking and entering at night, I wouldn't have a clue to where he slept or if he even had his own room.

"Oliver and Trent are going to find you in a hot minute if you don't get a better hiding space." An acorn bounced off my shoulder and I looked up to see what could only be described as an angel perch on a tree branch. The setting sun cast a halo effect over her white-blonde hair. A radiant smile adorned her face until recognition set in. "You're not Tate. What the hell are you doing here?" She swung down from the tree and glared.

I'd seen her from afar last summer and thought Akela was going to be a beautiful woman. It was a gut punch to have her this close, though. She was at least four years younger than me, barely over fifteen, but that didn't matter to my wolf side. It recognized who she would be to me immediately. Tate's substitute sister was going to be my mate. I watched her eyes dilate as she took in a shuddering breath. She felt it too.

Tongue-tied, all I could do was reach for her. My hand landed on her shoulder and an electric spark tingled through my fingertips. Without conscious thought, I pulled her to me. She stumbled into my chest, befuddled but not resisting.

She shook her head looking to clear it. "What was that?" Her voice was shaky, as if she couldn't form a proper thought.

I angled my head down and buried my nose in her hair. She smelled like sunshine and green things. My scenting spooked her. She pulled back looking up at me. I couldn't let her run away until we at least spoke about it. Her eyes grew wide as I opened my mouth, fear settled in those blue depths, and my heart broke to see it. I slid my hand to the side of her face attempting to comfort her. I wanted to tell her she had nothing to fear from me.

Out of nowhere a large shape tackled me from the side. Before I could even register my brother's face, he delivered a punch right to my mouth. "Fuck you!" he screamed. "You don't touch her. Ever!"

I shoved Tate off me before he could wind up and hit me again. Akela had stepped away covering her face with her hands. "Damn it, Tate. I didn't do anything to her." I stood up dusting myself off.

Tate stayed kneeling on the ground, panting and shooting daggers at me. "That's a lie. She looked frightened! You piece of filth! Your hands were all over her."

Even though the Greys were bigger and stronger, the Reds always acted like they were better than us, and now, my baby brother was no exception. "She's my mate," I spat out, the blood pooling in my mouth from the fat lip he'd given me. "We both felt the beginning connection."

Tate looked at me with extreme doubt. Akela flat out denied me. "No. I felt no such thing." The look of disgust on her face told me what I already knew. She thought I was a worthless piece of shit too. The thing was, she was right. I almost killed my own father. I'd hardly a dime to my name. No idea about the future. She was still just a kid. I needed to drive away and never look back. She was better without me.

"All right then." I held up my hands. Tate's glare stopped me from ever asking him if he wanted to leave with me. It was clear he never would have said yes anyway. He thought the worst of me. He was one of them now. "You can both go to hell."

Chapter Seven

Present Day

I rested my hand on the small of Akela's back while I walked her up the front stairs. She was tense. I wasn't sure if it was from our physical contact, or if she was steadying herself to meet the pack. I swung open the door with one hand, but the other refused to stop touching my mate. It had been six months since I was with her last and I was aching. I could see her pulse fluttering on her delicate neck, yet by all other outward appearances she was stoic, almost bored, as she stepped through the door. Between the two of us, I was definitely more nervous. I might've blackmailed her into being here, but everything was riding on her choice to stay. I tried to see the pack and our place through her eyes and gauge her reaction.

The cabin was old but well kept. I was damn handy with woodwork as well as cars. Fixing up old things was what I did best. Our place certainly did look rustic, nothing like the kind of modern home I pictured Akela growing up in. The furniture was mismatched, faded rugs covered the wood floors, and decorations were sparse. An old handmade picture frame hung slightly crooked above the fireplace. Inside was a picture taken at the all-pack summer gathering of a group of kids. One rare moment of a bunch of us laughing. Akela and Tate were only a few feet away from me and it was the only photo I had of them. A half-dead houseplant sat on the kitchen table, courtesy of this old lady that brought me random things every oil change. Basically, the only new thing in the entire place was the television—something the entire pack agreed was a necessity.

The guys were crowded in the living room watching a game when we stepped in. I did a quick count, all but Dex had made it. As soon as I ushered Akela inside, they all sprung up from the couch and shut off the game. I almost smiled at the reaction. They certainly never jumped up to greet me. Convincing my mate to stay and accept us was a priority we all shared.

I cleared my throat praying this would go off without a hitch. Hell, I'd settle for the guys not embarrassing me or Akela not being a cold bitch. "Akela," I spoke in my most welcoming tone. "This is the pack." They lined up for introductions without me needing to say any more.

"This is Luke," I gestured to the man with eyes the color of storm clouds. Luke was as pale as a marble statue with muscles as hard as rocks. He didn't look like any of the Wa'ya from this region.

"It's nice to formally meet you." Luke reached out his hand and Akela took it without hesitation.

"I've seen you around town. You're not a Grey," she stated while peering intently at him.

"No, I'm not." He rubbed the back of his neck. "I'm an arctic wolf. My pack was slaughtered a few years back. I was the only one left. Traveled out of Alaska needing a change. Found Miles that same year and decided to stay. Felt right."

My jaw almost dropped open. Luke was extremely quiet and pensive. It had taken me four months to learn his story. I'd never heard him put so many words together on a first introduction. It took him years to build up enough trust to have a full conversation with anyone. The fact he offered up all that information to Akela in a few seconds was telling. He was lonely and feeling isolated, only an alpha female could change things for him.

Akela's expression was solemn as she regarded him. I burned to know what she was thinking. "It's nice to meet you as well, Luke. I'm truly sorry to hear about your former pack." Luke nodded at her condolences before Akela acknowledged Caius. Her mouth puckered and drew in tight. "Abduct any other women today, Caius?"

I held my breath. Akela had met him years ago, long before I asked him to help abduct Chloe. We had a few dive bar hopping nights out together. Caius was known for having an incredibly short fuse and crass mouth. I'm hardly one to judge, but women often commented on how beautiful he was. The ladies always flocked to him at the clubs over the rest of us. Until he spoke, that is. Nights either ended with a firm slap across the face or a quickie in the bathroom. He was prettier, that's for sure. They would gush over his smooth complexion and thick black curls. He was perfectly proportioned like a superhero. In a party setting, he was all right. Alcohol removed his sharp edges. Sober, he was a mean son of a bitch with an enormous chip on his shoulder courtesy of his former pack.

"Nope," his square jaw ground to the left as he spoke.

My Viking goddess crossed her arms over her chest. "Got anything else to say?" She stared into his eyes, a direct challenge. I started to hold up my hand, thinking he would need me to calm him down, when he answered.

"I wish that shit hadn't gone down." He chewed on his lip and jutted his head at me. "Alpha seemed to be out of options, though. I did what we had to for the pack."

She squinted slightly and nodded. "Fair enough. I won't bust your balls for his actions." She jutted her thumb in my direction. One might think I'd be sore at Caius for selling me out, but I was relieved he kept his cool. It was a rare thing. Akela was already having a good effect on him.

I watched my mate instinctually change her demeanor when facing my next pack member. Her lips titled in the first smile and her eyes warmed. Kyle shuffled closer and sheepishly held out a hand. His smell was a mixture of patchouli oil and skunky weed. The kid was rail thin and his shaggy brown hair covered most of his eyes giving him a boyish appearance. He was the only member of my pack that Akela had never seen before.

"Hey." He shook her hand repeatedly before letting it go. "I'm Kyle. Welcome home."

Instead of responding to him, her searching ocean-blue eyes landed on me. "You really do have an omega in your pack."

It wasn't a question, but I knew what my girl was asking. Why would I, an alpha from a pack that hated all shows of weakness, have an omega member when there was not yet a need for one?

"Don't let the baby face fool you, Kyle carries more than his fair share around here. He stays in the cabin year-round, prepping for our monthly visits, on top of being one of the highest income earners for the pack." I slapped his shoulder while he blushed at the praise.

A full smile graced Akela's lips showing off her perfect little dimple. Alpha females always loved the omegas best. The rare exception being my mother, who was incapable of that emotion. "What do you do?" she asked.

"Web designer." Kyle puffed up a bit, obviously pleased by her attention. "Easy to work remote. No one notices the strange hours I like to keep. My only big splurges are a new MacBook every few years and the best Wi-Fi we can get."

"You don't get lonely here between full moons?" she asked sweetly, her tone reflecting true concern.

Kyle shrugged. "Of course, but I like to grow things. Most of our food comes from my garden. Keeps me occupied when the work is slow."

"I'd love to see it. My folks farm too. Growing things is in the blood."

"I could take you now," Kylie responded with the eagerness of a young pup despite being only a year younger than Akela.

I chuckled. "Best wait till tomorrow, when the sun is out, man."

Akela winked at him. "It's a date." My heart swelled at the gesture. Things were going better than expected.

"This wannabe punk here is Able." With his spiky mohawk, black skinny jeans, ripped leather jacket adorned with hundreds of safety pins, scuffed Doc Martens, and a British flag wristband, he looked like he should be on an album cover. Able may not have been alive during the eighties, but his presence personified the decade.

"You a Dead Kennedys fan?" Akela asked looking at his tee.

"You heard of them?" Able perked up at his favorite topic.

"Oh, yeah, my mom was a crazy fan. She even convinced my dad to take a trip to Cambodia because of their music." She laughed easily and Able instantly became as enchanted with her as I was.

"Holiday in Cambodia. Classic." He grinned.

"You seem familiar. Have we met?" Her brow furrowed as she puzzled it out. Akela and I had a memorable encounter at a convenience store while Able was stealing liquor inside. The kid had some sticky fingers. Not wanting her to puzzle it out too soon, I thrust her in front of Xan.

Xan was the most notable Native American in my pack... Most Greys had some shared lineage mixed with Wa'ya packs that migrated here from other continents. There were many Greys that were Eurasian wolves in origin, along with Eastern and Tundra wolves, they tended to favor more European in appearance. Xan grew up on tribal lands and could trace his lineage back hundreds of years. He was forced to leave his pack when it became unstable. The lack of female alphas that could shift was causing packs that had alpha pairs to swell too large. Large packs could not go undetected. That was unsafe for many reasons. Xan's former pack was forced to send their young males out in hopes of them finding other packs to join. That was how he had found me. He was one of the few of us that didn't have a fucked-up family story. His family was cool, and helped us out when they could. It was always great when we could manage to spend time with them.

Thick black hair fell to the center of his back, yet he kept the sides over his ears shaved. Unlike Caius, who once he opened his mouth propelled people away like magnets, Xan was a charmer. He possessed a swagger that had the girls falling over themselves to sleep with him. I half expected him to be eye-fucking my mate. Luckily for him, the interest I saw sparkling from his dark-brown eyes appeared purely platonic.

"Please don't get him started talking about music," Xan played at being pained. "Or else I will never get to say hello. I'm Xan in case you didn't remember.."

"We have crossed paths a few times at Cheers and Beers. Of course, I remember you." She rolled her eyes at him.

I groaned out loud before she said more. "Please tell me you didn't hit on her."

Akela looked at me sharply, her lip twitching in annoyance. "No, he didn't. He was with you all three times. First time was my twenty-first birthday. I'm sure you recall *that* night?"

Realization dawned on me then. I hadn't remembered the name of the bar since it had changed owners. It was the place she used to frequent often until she realized I was stalking her there. Xan smoothed over the awkward moment.

"You were doing shots faster than the DJ changed songs that night. So I wasn't sure if my name stuck." His most charming smile was produced solely for her.

It might have been slightly forced, but she managed to smile back and shake off another memory I would give anything to take back. "Well, we are officially acquainted now."

"Are you tired from the drive? We can put a pot of coffee on for you? Or maybe a beer if you want to chill a bit?" Xan played the attentive host, but it was Kyle that ran to the kitchen looking stricken.

"Ah, man, so rude not to offer you anything when you came in. We all just converged on you," he said and grimaced.

Akela waved him back. "I'm good, thanks. Go ahead and turn back on the game. I'm always happy to watch the Volunteers lose."

Xan howled with laughter. "Uh-oh, Caius, Akela just threw down some fighting words."

Caius's mouth was screwed up tight. Dude was trying to stay on his best behavior. Akela took pity on him with a slap on the shoulder. "No worries, man, there are worse things to butt heads on."

His lips turned up on one side and I released a breath I hadn't realized I'd been holding. "You're on then!" Caius crowed. "This is Tennessee's year for sure."

The jovial rivalry was shattered when the front door banged open and Dex walked in. Akela's hackles were immediately up. She'd never liked Dex. I knew this part wasn't going to go as smoothly as everything else had.

"Well, well , well," he leered. "The perfect pack princess has decided to grace us with her presence. What's the deal? Thought you might want to see how the other half lived?"

"Dex!" The growl in my voice was pure alpha. "You were warned."

I sighed as the unhappy pinched expression returned to Akela's features. One step forward and Dex took us two steps back. "If I'm not wanted…" she trailed off.

I removed any space between us and blocked Dex from her line of sight. My hand settled on her hip. "I'm one hundred percent certain I could not possibly want you more."

I saw the spark of interest flare to life in her eyes. Her cheeks heated to a beautiful shade of pink. I was about to throw her over my shoulder caveman style and carry her away, but my damn beta couldn't keep his mouth shut.

"Don't get too cozy, gang. Princess here will split the first chance she gets. She refuses to see us as anything more than scum." Dex, by far the biggest man in the room, besides me, folded his arm over his chest and glared at my girl. If he wasn't my oldest friend, that action alone would be enough for me to all-out attack him.

Akela wasn't one to be intimidated. Her instincts

were pure alpha. She stepped away from me, directly facing off against Dex. "Well, if it smells like shit and looks like shit, it generally is a piece of shit," she spat venom, eyes flashing like blue angry flames.

He took an angry step toward her. I was about to pound on his ass if he didn't get in line right away. Surprisingly, Caius defused the situation.

"Oh, fucking chill, Dex! We were about to get back to the game. If you're going to talk out of your ass, do it somewhere else." Caius picked up the remote, turned the volume way up, and plopped down on the couch.

"Beers?" Kyle rummaged in the kitchen fridge pulling out a twelve pack. He handed Akela and I the first cans before setting the rest on the coffee table for the guys to help themselves. Akela played it cool, taking a sip of her beer and claiming my La-Z-Boy. She didn't spare Dex another glance. I waited, my eyes boring into his, indicating I would not tolerate any more. Dex ground his teeth, snatched a beer from the table, and headed to the room he shared with Luke.

I physically hoisted Akela up, stole her spot, and positioned her on my lap. I held onto her hips firmly, fully expecting resistance or a slap. When she remained on my lap after little more than an annoyed huff, a warm fuzzy glow erupted from my chest. She was doing what she promised when she traded herself for Chloe. She was giving us a chance.

All things considered, I'd say it was going quite well.

Chapter Eight

Ten Years Ago

Being a lone wolf wasn't as terrible as I'd thought it would be. I'd never traveled before. My entire life mainly took place in a twenty-mile radius of the house I was born in. In the three years since I left my family, I'd backpacked up and down both the East and West Coast. Hikers were a friendly laid-back lot, very generous, and never suspicious of a kid who hadn't seen indoor plumbing in a while.

With humans, my size always made me a standout. I would take any odd jobs that required serious strength like chopping wood, hauling others' gear to campsites, or wildfire volunteering. Finally, I landed a gig as a trail worker. The pay was crap but my expenses were low and the hours around my shifting manageable. Carrying a fifty-pound pack and hiking ten to fifteen miles each day was a breeze for me. It also made me feel good about myself, a total novelty. People would constantly stop and thank me for my work. They saw me as a conservationist doing my part to keep our planet healthy. It wasn't the exact truth as to why I was out alone for days in the wild, but it felt damn delightful being looked at like one of the good guys.

I was solitary most of my days, though. My wolf loved being outdoors. The novelty eventually wore off for my human side. I missed hot meals, beds with pillows, and football. Mainly the need to see Akela again was the force that had me shifting my course toward home. My supervisor was a solid guy, might also have been under the impression I was an orphan on account I'd never once mentioned my folks. When I told him I was heading back to Tennessee, he gave me the contact of his uncle Doug who owned a repair shop. Because Doug's arthritis was getting bad, he was looking for help around the shop. I was the handyman around here when anything needed fixing, so he felt confident about putting in a good word for me.

Doug was even more decent than his nephew. Gave me a job over the phone and a room to rent over his shop. There was no reason not to return. I wasn't a piece of shit, people liked me, and I'd have a job and a home. Akela was eighteen now. I fantasized about what she'd be doing and how it would be to see her again.

A week after I settled in and things were working out at the garage, I reached out to my friend Dex. He was super pumped to hear from me and we agreed to meet at the bar down the corner to catch up. I was curious about pack life. It may not have been an idyllic childhood, but my wolf side missed the connections.

Dex was already in the bar finishing off his first beer when I arrived. He stood up and slapped my shoulder with a bit more force than a normal hello. It was a dominance play, but I didn't flinch. Dex might be almost as big as me, but he was still a beta. No chance for him to take me in a fight either human or wolf. I grasped his shoulder in a squeeze forcing him back onto his stool. There was no other response to offer, my alpha side couldn't shrug off a challenge. Part of me was disappointed Dex tried that crap, though. I'd forgotten the constant requirement the pack put on me to prove my worth.

"Dang, man," Dex grimaced as he rubbed his shoulder. "You been out lifting rocks for the last few years?"

He was spot-on. Clearing falling rocks and boulders from trails was a big part of what I used to do. "What's your problem, man? Forgot you weren't the alpha?" I chuckled with little warmth. It had only taken a few seconds and I'd fallen back too quickly into the role of supreme dick.

Dex didn't seem to mind. In fact, my attitude had him perking up. "So, are you back to take on your pops, then? Man, it is going to be so sweet to be buds with 'the' alpha."

"Nah, man," I huffed. "I'm not interested in that job."

"Why the hell come back, then?" Dex looked legitimately confused.

It felt wrong to tell him about Akela. "Just thought it was time to check on things."

"You are checking up on a pack you have no intention of leading?" he asked with disdain.

"I'm still young, bro. No need to tie myself to a full-time lifelong job." I signaled the bartender to bring two more beers.

Dex waited till the old man deposited them and walked away. "I can respect that, man." He grinned. "Living large and chasing tail." He held up his hand for a high five that I grudgingly reciprocated. "My mom has an absolutely shit fit if she hears I went to town. I'm twenty-one years old and she's on me all the time about staying away from the human girls, they're beneath me. But that's exactly where I want them to be. Am I right?" He offered another high-five request that I answered with an eye roll. He shrugged and powered on. "But seriously, not sure what she expects? There are hardly any girls that aren't broken, and the good ones all go for alphas."

Broken. That was how most packs saw the shiftless females being born. I was extremely grateful that wasn't Akela's situation. I wondered about her. Our connection sparked at such a young age, she must be a strong alpha. It's different with chicks, they don't try to kill each other like the male alphas do in wolf form, but for girls it's more difficult when human. Must make it hell to accept pack rules. The women tend to be total bitches to each other as the full moon approaches. It's a constant battle of wills. I wonder if she was forced to leave her pack. I hoped since she wasn't born a Grey that wasn't the case. Reds were usually more nurturing. The idea that she wasn't where I expected her to be, left a rock in my stomach and caused me to miss a few things Dex was saying. The overall gist was he couldn't stand his mom.

"Why not move out, then?" I asked.

He got quiet and appeared uncomfortable. "I was hoping you were coming back. Thought it might change the dynamics at home if you were running things. But I'll just join your pack until you're ready for the big show."

"Hold up, bro. I don't have a pack. I live the life of a lone wolf."

"Then we can be lone wolves together," he said and shrugged. "It's not natural to be on your own for so long."

I hesitated instead of immediately rejecting his idea. Dex was the only wolf I'd known that offered to sever pack bonds and join me. It wasn't a small sacrifice. He might be over his mom nagging him, but that woman cared for him. Unlike my own mother, who would sooner see the life leave my eyes if I wasn't an alpha as tough as her. "Are you serious? Breaking the pack bonds will be painful."

"I'm twenty-one and still being treated like I'm thirteen. Away from the pack I can do shit! Eat what I want. Go where I feel like being. Bagging babes and taking charge. How about that one?" He wiggled his bushy eyebrows causing me to laugh.

"Think it over more. Once my mom releases you,

there's no take-backs." I didn't want my loneliness to override my common sense. Dex leaving would mean he was my responsibility as an alpha. I was touched by his offer, but we both should consider if it was a good choice.

Dex's face became pinched. "She already did."

"What?"

He shrugged again but with much less indifference. "I told your mom I was meeting up with you."

"Why?" I asked truly bewildered.

"She saw me a few months back and asked if I had heard from you. I made the alpha a promise that I'd inform her if I did. Might have told her we talked about me being your beta one day back when we were kids." He shrugged it off as if informing me that brownnosing my crazy mom was a normal thing.

"What did she say to that?"

"She told me to get my car packed and think about leaving. That you might need backup out there on the road," he replied strangely proud.

"But you didn't come and join me," I stated the obvious.

"Well, not then, when you were living like a wild animal in the middle of nowhere. But as soon as you got back, I packed up the car and told her I was ready. She released me of the bond then and there. Said she would put it back up once I brought you home." He took a slow swig of his beer waiting for my reaction.

"I told you, I am not going back."

"Hey, brother..." Dex saluted me with two fingers. "Bachelor pad living it is, then. I'm here to be your wingman."

"Wow." I swallowed unsure how to process this huge shift in my future. The idea of having to suddenly watch out for another. The alpha in me was greedy for it. I personally was a bit wary. "Do you have a place to stay?"

Dex shook his head. Sighing, I pulled out my phone to call Doug. He had another room for rent. Maybe this was fate. Guess I was starting my own pack.

Three days later I cosigned a lease for Dex and got him situated. He ate like the rabid animal he was, forcing me out on my second grocery run in a week. He only had a few hundred dollars on him, and with his eating habits it wouldn't last long. It was time to find him a job. As we entered Publix I noticed a HELP WANTED sign for a nighttime restock clerk. Our kind are naturally night owls, so while Dex went to fill out an application. I grabbed a shopping cart and started down the aisles.

I hadn't built up the nerve to see Akela. She was on my mind far more than my brother these days. The mating bond can be a real bitch if denied. I was barely sleeping these days. My anxiety was off the charts. I needed a fix. I needed to see her. As if my intense desire had created a magnetic pull, I heard a feminine intake of breath behind me that had all the fine hairs on my neck standing at attention. I whipped around.

My beautiful porcelain-skinned doll stood mute before me. I didn't mind. It gave me more time to drink her in. She had grown taller in the last three years, all legs. She changed her golden-blonde ringlets. It was iron-straight platinum-blonde now with hot pink at the tip, just long enough to cover fully developed breasts.

Her mouth opened and closed a few times as if she planned to speak. I hated how awkward it was between us. How sluggish and limp our bond felt. I took pity on her. "Hey, Akela, you here shopping?"

My question shocked her out of whatever stupor she was trapped in. "It's been a long time," she whispered. "Are you back?"

My heart soared that she cared to ask, yet something about the soft question rattled me. She would always be striking even covered in dirt, but I noticed dark circles under her eyes, her nails looked chewed on, and she nibbled constantly on chapped lips. All signs her wolf had been pining for its mate. Thank the Maker she wasn't shiftless. If that was the case, she would happily have gone on ignoring me forever. There might be hope for us yet.

I had to touch her. My hand touched her shoulder, little electric zings grazing my skin, while I grabbed a lock of her hair. "I like the look. Makes me wonder if you might have a pink-tinged tail?"

She didn't jerk away or scowl. We were definitely making progress. Her cheeks warmed to a delicate shade of dusty rose under my scrutiny. "Thanks."

"And to answer your question. I am back. I wanted to give you time, but three years is all I could manage."

Her open expression shuddered. She licked dry lips and looked down. "Look, Miles—"

I cut her off not liking the direction of her tone. "Did you tell Tate the truth? Or does he still think of me as a complete ass?"

She snorted. "Well, aren't ya still?"

I leaned in, caging her effectively with my arms and a wall of canned vegetables. "Never to you."

Her eyes darted around my face. "I'm truly not sure what to make of you."

"We haven't given it much effort, yet. Meet me at the park tomorrow?" I asked.

"Can't." She shook her head.

I frowned. "Why not?"

"It's my graduation." She smiled at my obvious confusion. "You know, cap and gown and all that stuff."

"Weren't you just homeschooled?"

"Sure, but we still had interactions and small group learning sessions. There will be fifty other kids graduating. Only two of us are Wa'ya, the rest human."

"Did Tate have a real graduation too?" I liked and hated the thought all at once. Jealousy mixed with pride at my baby bro.

"Of course, every kid in Austin's pack does."

I pulled away and held out my hand. "Can I put my number in your phone?"

She didn't hesitate and my heart rate doubled. I decided to leave out my name and simply type *Mate*. It would be under M so when she looked for Miles, she would find it. I hoped she wouldn't change it. I was just finishing entering my number when Dex found us.

"Damn, Miles, you never even look at a girl in the bars. I leave you for twenty minutes and come back to find you slumming it." Dex laughed expecting me to join in until he noticed me handing back Akela's phone. "What's going on here?"

"None of your damn business." Akela roughly shoved the phone in her back pocket and glared.

"Don't disrespect her," I growled.

Dex's eyes went wide. "A Fuckin' Red! No way, man. You're not only going to have to take out your dad but your momma as well. No way is she letting you take over the pack if this bitch is your mate."

"Watch it!" I tried not to raise my voice, humans were noticing us.

Horror washed over Akela's features before she settled on disgust. "Figures," she spit out. "The company you keep says a lot about who you are." With that parting shot she stormed off before I could stop her.

"Good riddance, man! Best keep this on the down-low or you'll lose all the Greys' respect." He punched my arm in a brotherly fashion and I wanted to literally strangle him in return. "Props to me, though. Totally landed this gig. I start Monday."

It had been going so well! I wanted to pull my hair out. Or possibly remove my only pack mate's tongue. I couldn't fault him totally. Years of living in my former pack meant hating Reds on sight. I'd played along for years, not wanting to feel Momma's disapproval. "Great news, you can cover the groceries, then."

With my hands curled in fists and my teeth tightly clenched I walked out.

Chapter Nine

Seven Years Ago

It wasn't natural for a true mate to be rejected. It happened, of course. Our human sides made poor choices, acted irrationally, or were just plain stubborn. My mate was the latter. It broke something to have her avoid me at every chance encounter, or worse, eye-fuck me like crazy from across a room then reject me if I came near. It did things to me, hardened me. She expected this evil asshole because of my former pack, never giving me a chance. Tonight, I was going to give her what she expected. Tonight, I wasn't going to meekly walk away and allow her to ignore me.

It was Akela's twenty-first birthday and there were only two places she would be heading out to celebrate. I intended to party crash. She was making my life a living hell and I'd be damned if she got to have a perfect night with her perfect friends and perfect family. My mood was leaking out and affecting the guys around me. They started drinking heavily as soon as we hit the first potential club. My busted-up ragtag pack wasn't just Dex and me anymore. Apparently, I was an asshole magnet and I had a soft spot for jerks no one else wanted. Caius was certainly pretty on the outside but he had a temper like a tornado.

A few months back, I woke up after a shift with Caius passed out a few feet away. He looked beat to shit. I thought my wolf must not have accepted him, but after he grumbled his name, he offered an excuse for his unexpected black-and-blue presence. His old pack had beat him to an inch of his life then cast him out. The change happened while he was alone in the woods and his wolf must have found us. I've been stuck with him ever since.

Two rounds of beers and shots went down quickly. I didn't see Akela but it was only nine, she may not have made it out yet. We could hang back a few before we bounced and tried the next place. The guys knew I was here to corner my girl tonight and they were just the crew to accompany me.

"Hey…" Dex pointed at a guy playing pool by himself. He had thick black hair that fell past his shoulders covering his face as he leaned in for the shot. "That's the guy I met at the market. He's *new* in town."

The meaningful way Dex spoke was code for lone wolf. I looked at the man a little closer. He was tall and bulky, most likely a Grey. His arms were covered in deep-navy markings barely visible over his dark-brown skin. Some packs out West used markings to tell the history of their pack, but I didn't recognize his symbols. I took a few steps closer before I breathed out. Not an alpha, but his energies were strong, most likely a beta.

His coffee-colored eyes jerked up when he sensed my presence. A nod of the head and the lowering of his eyes indicated he was no threat. "Up for a game?" I asked when I stopped next to the table. There was a beat of silence as he regarded me. Not wanting to scare him off, I held out my hand. "I'm Miles."

A slow smile spread across his face revealing perfectly white teeth. "Name's Xan." He looked around seeing how close the humans might be. "It's been a while since I've seen a pack. Heard there were a few out these parts, though."

Dex grabbed a stick and chalked up. "If you want to see other wolves, you came to the right place, man. At least three main packs frequent here. This is what we call the neutral zone."

Caius racked up the balls, interrupting Xan's

game without asking. "I think of it more of the hookup spot myself," he leered. "Human girls aplenty if you can't find the right tail, if you know what I mean."

Xan took our muscling in on his spot in stride. "I'm a bit of a drifter myself, but it's nice to sense other Wa'ya. Females would be preferred, though." He chuckled.

"Why are you away from your pack then?" I questioned.

"Grew too large," Xan sighed. "With no new alpha pairs in the area to break up our numbers. I volunteered to leave for pack safety."

I nodded my acceptance of his statement. It was common to hear. Packs were either dwindling with no females able to shift, or swelling with no new alpha couples emerging to split packs up. Packs getting too large were bad for business, increased the risk of getting caught, made hunting grounds overused, and often drew in poachers. In short, packs with over fifty shifters spelled out danger. Pack bonds became unstable. When bonds were not strong, many young men in their early twenties were filled with restless energy, causing them to wander. Either they found another pack, found a mate, or stayed a lone wolf unable to ever settle.

"Are we playing or not?" Caius complained. The man knew nothing of patience.

I pulled another stick off the wall. "Let's shoot some pool."

Caius broke and sunk the four-ball in. "Solids," he called out.

Xan watched Caius move around the table to get to his next shot. "Are you part of a larger pack?"

I shook my head. "Just the three of us."

"Our old pack is about a few hours' north." Dex grimaced. "But I'm sure you can tell Miles here is an alpha. Dude is always pushing out serious waves of energy. Since his pop is still alpha there, we aren't heading back quite yet."

"I heard a rumor this was close to Red territory?" Xan probed.

Caius missed his next shot and cursed. Xan stepped up and hit the eleven and twelve balls in quick succession.

"That's why we're here." Dex had a bit of an evil gleam in his eye. "Miles's mate won't accept him and the dude is a glutton for punishment."

"Watch it, Dex," I warned.

The announcement I had a mate caused Xan to miss his next shot. "Wow, you found your true mate?" His interest level in me skyrocketed. I could feel him taking in my measure.

"Alpha Austin's niece turned twenty-one today. We are here to liven up the party," Caius said and grinned. "So, there should be plenty of she-wolves in one of these bars tonight."

The way Dex and Caius both laughed sowed a few seeds of doubt about me bringing them along. "I'll not ask you to keep your dick in your pants, Caius." I gave him a pointed look. "But please don't tell any of them they're your mates."

"Hey," Caius said, shrugging. "You never know till you try, right?"

Xan raised an eyebrow looking puzzled. Dex howled with laughter. "Caius is truly brilliant. In his last pack he went to all the shiftless females and told them he felt the mate bond and just like that,"—he snapped—"they all jumped into bed with him."

Our new friend looked a bit bothered hearing about the act of feigning one of our most sacred things. Made him rise more in my opinion. "That couldn't have ended well?"

"Nah…" Caius had the grace to look sheepish. "Got me beaten and kicked out of my old pack." The grin reemerged while he spoke. "But it was a hell of a way to go!"

The front door opened with a riot of female laughter. The constant ache in my chest lessoned minutely. My mate was nearby.

"Hot damn," Dex shouted gleefully. "Let the games begin."

Turning slowly, I zeroed in on my prey. It felt like my tongue swelled in my mouth, I was finding it hard to swallow. Akela was wearing a short slinky dress that reminded me of a rainbow-colored oil slick. The tight black shiny number barely covered her ass, showcasing mouthwatering toned long legs. It had a high neck held on to her body by a flimsy gold choker. The entirety of her back was exposed. I was torn between admiring what was mine and wanting to rip out every human male's eyes that ogled her.

Her friends were cute, but not Akela's level of hot. Two brunettes and one strawberry-blonde were also dressed as if this was Las Vegas. None of them had Akela's alpha confidence or came close to her beauty. Barring a Victoria Secret runway model, not many could compare to my Viking goddess. Her friends headed straight for the bar, but Akela placed her hand over her heart and searched the place with wild eyes.

I froze completely when they landed on me. I could see her nipples pebble under the thin fabric of the halter dress, her breathing turned heavy as her chest lifted and fell in the most mesmerizing way. She unconsciously licked her lips. I went rock-hard instantly imagining that sweet mouth covering me.

"Get your ass over here, girl, and take a shot with

us!" the strawberry-blonde hollered, oblivious of me and the other Wa'ya in the room. It was enough to shake Akela out of our moment. She turned away without acknowledging me yet again.

"I sure as hell don't see the ice queen you keep mentioning," Caius breathed out shaking his hand like he touched something hot. "The heat coming off her stare could light a fire."

"What are you talking about?" scoffed Dex. "That bitch disrespected him yet again."

I was going to tell Dex to shut the hell up about my mate, when surprisingly, Xan did it for me. "That seems a bit unfair, man. She's young. Female alphas are not always ready as early as male alphas to leave their home pack. Clearly, she has feelings for you, Miles. If that's your true mate, it's just a matter of time."

"Maybe…" I pursed my lips. "But I feel like I've waited long enough already." I sized up Xan. "There are four of them and four of us. Looks like fate invited us to the party." I felt a predatory smile split my face.

I didn't wait for an answer. I turned and sauntered over to the bar. My alpha pull would most likely have all the guys following behind me. As much as we were individuals, we were also a pack like people. It was hard to go against our natural inclinations. My instincts, right now, were telling me to go and lay claim.

I watched the girls clink their glasses together and down the first shot. Akela grimaced and covered her mouth. "That was awful." She giggled. "What was that?"

The shortest brunette answered, "Jägermeister! It's my favorite."

"It tasted like cough syrup mixed with moonshine," she said pretending to gag. "Do not order that for me again."

I reached her then. My hand splayed across all

that exposed skin on her lower back. She tensed up immediately when I leaned in to whisper, "Allow me to buy you a drink."

"That won't be…" She started to reject me, but I cut her off.

"Bartender!" I signaled. "We'll take eight B-52 shots."

Akela glared at me, but her friends were making appreciative eyes at Pretty Boy Caius and Xan. Dex was a mean-looking son of a bitch and tended to frighten most everyone on first inspection. He continued to hold back and glower.

"Listen, it's just us ladies tonight," Akela started but her friends quickly chimed in.

"We can make an exception, of course, if you continue to buy the drinks." She batted her eyes at me. I inspected the girls closer then, they were not from Austin's pack, but rather from a few other packs located farther away. Friends Akela probably made at the summer gatherings, and less likely to hate me on sight like her family would.

"Darling, I do believe that can be arranged as long as the birthday girl agrees to dance with me." My hand slid from touching her back to curling around her waist and drawing her closer to my side.

The other girls cheered when the shots arrived. "Pretty!" the strawberry-blonde exclaimed. "Look at the three layers in the glass all separated! How do they do that?"

"Well…" Caius leaned in and handed the girl a glass. "I can't tell you how it works but I can show you the best way to take a shot. You put your lips all around the edge and seal them real tight, then drop your head back and swallow."

I groaned outwardly, while the brunettes giggled

at his vulgarity. The blonde was ready to party. "You mean like this." She slowly raised the glass to her lips and practically deep-throated the dang thing before tipping her head back and downing the shot. She finished by slamming down the empty glass on the bar and daintily wiping the sides of her mouth with just her pinky.

Caius's jaw actually dropped. "Marry me."

The girl stuck out her tongue and slapped him playfully on the shoulder. "Let's just start with a dance, Pretty Boy." She grabbed his hand and pulled him toward the dance floor, leaving the rest of us to grab our shots without them.

"Cheers to the lovely birthday girl," I shouted over the music. Everyone took a drink, and I watched Akela look at her glass warily before she knocked it back. Her eyes lit up when she was done.

"That was actually good," she sounded pleasantly relieved.

I leaned in close, speaking so only she could hear, "I could make many things good if you would only give me the chance."

She sucked in a breath and swallowed. Her ocean-blue eyes devoured my face with as much longing as I felt every day for her. My original plan for the night was to ruin her evening by sticking to her side like glue weather she liked it or not. Change of plans! My girl was acting like she was ready to be seduced.

My lips drifted softly over her ear. "Dance with me." It wasn't a request, but she still nodded dreamily, the shots loosening up her normally rigid attitude.

When we reached the dance floor, a fast techno beat thumped through the room. I ignored it completely and brought her body in flush against mine. Dancing with her slowly, I leaned down and nuzzled my face on the side of hers. In the six years I'd known Akela was my mate, this was the first time I'd held her for more than a few seconds. My heart was beating faster than the music. The constant ache in my chest from being far from her finally dissipated. She sighed at the same time I did. She'd felt it too. I wanted to demand why she fought so hard against this, but knew it would end this moment of peace if I did.

One song faded into another and we continued to sway. Her arms circled around my back and she rested against my chest. Even wearing three-inch heels, she was still at least a half-foot shorter than me. I'd never seen her as delicate, yet as I held her all I could think about was how I would make sure nothing and no one would ever hurt her. My hand skated down her spine causing her breath to shudder, before I rested it on the small of her back just above the curve of her firm ass.

That moment was pure heaven, at least until her girlfriends found us. The strawberry-blonde was dragging Caius in our direction as the two brunettes stepped right up beside us. A quick glance back showed that Dex and Xan stayed at the bar. It was too much for me to hope that Dex could keep the ladies entertained. No one would call him a charmer.

"What music are the two of you listening to?" one of her friends laugh-shouted at us.

Akela pulled away. A lovely pink blush settled on her cheeks as she blinked and took in the scene around us. A mixture of intense pride and profound anger hit me. My mate had found simple bliss just being in my arms. She had even forgotten for a moment where she was. It changed nothing, though. She took a few steps away and laughed apologetically to the girls, while avoiding looking into my eyes. I knew she was more embarrassed that she felt that bliss with me than zoning out on the dance floor.

The tallest brunette had brought her another shot that looked like a lemon drop. I should have asked for their names earlier, but the moment had passed. Akela knocked it back smiling at her friend. I worried all the mixing would affect her later, but that's what twenty-first birthdays were all about. She started dancing alongside her friends, Caius signaled he was heading toward the bar. I leaned down so Akela could hear.

"I'm going to get you a water," I spoke loudly over the music.

"Boo!" heckled the strawberry-blonde. "Your boy is getting rum and cokes! That's all the water she needs."

The girls started grinding on each other and giggling, not in a super-sexy porn star way. They were genuinely sillier about it, like a parody of being in a music video. Akela had never looked more adorable. I hadn't known she even possessed a goofy side.

Caius was making his way back from the bar juggling four rum and cokes in clear plastic cups. Xan trailed behind with three beers. The girls cheered when they took the beverages. I chuckled wondering how much they would regret this bender tomorrow. Caius grabbed a beer from Xan and started trying to insert himself between the girls hoping they would then grind on him. I rolled my eyes. The dude was shameless.

"Thanks, man." I knocked bottles with Xan as he nodded in response to the offering. His eyes strayed to my woman and I stiffened a little until he spoke.

"Congrats on finding you true mate, man," he spoke quietly. "Dex says she can shift too."

"Did he also gripe about her being a Red?" I asked.

Xan scoffed. "Who the fuck would care about that? You can have a real pack. I've known alpha males turned lone wolves because they never found 'the one,' and yours is right in front of you." He slapped my shoulder as if I'd accomplished a great feat.

"She keeps running from me," I grumbled the awkward truth.

Xan flashed his toothy smile. "Wolves do like to be chased, man."

"Ain't that the truth," I muttered.

Akela was surely tipsy, but not quite drunk. It took a little more alcohol to put our kind flat on our asses. She looked my way with a flirty smile while she shook her hips. I took a long sip of my beer and handed it back to Xan. "Here goes nothing, then."

It hadn't taken much to convince Akela to step away with me for a break. She was glistening with perspiration, eyes slightly glazed from the combination of heat and drink. Instead of taking her outside like I had suggested, I pulled her into a large empty room the place used for private parties.

"I thought we were getting some air?" She glared at me, but in a playful way that encouraged me to keep directing her further into the vacant room.

"I'd say it's much cooler in here than on the dance floor. Besides, there will be a bunch of smokers hovering around the front door, and I know you hate that."

My comment surprised her. "You do?" A dreamy look flitted over her face.

"There is a great deal I still have to learn about you." I cradled her face between my hands. "Like what your lips will feel like when we kiss?" Her head stayed angled up and I took that for consent. The kiss started off gentle, but when she moaned and opened her mouth, all the suppressed sexual tension built up over the last couple of years burst like a broken damn.

We were devouring each other's mouths. Tongues evading, teeth clacking in our desire to be closer. My mate ripped the buttons off my shirt to get her hands over my chest. I reached around to grab her ass lifting her higher so I wasn't leaning down. She circled her legs around my waist and locked her hands behind my neck, all the while never stopping our kissing frenzy. The little black dress she wore rode up to her waist, exposing her bare ass to my touch and her little lace thong to my sight.

I carried her further into the room and set her down on a raised booth right on the edge of the table. Neither one of us spoke as my hand circled over her soaked panties and she whipped off my belt and unzipped my jeans. She reached in to touch me and I pushed aside her panties to feel the soft skin of her folds. Our stuttered breathing seemed loud in my ears making the music from the club feel farther away.

The last six years had felt like a curse. Men my age are sexually active constantly looking to score. I had met my mate when she was too young and was forced to walk away, but my body had stayed loyal. The thought of anyone else made me physically ill, forcing me to remain a virgin still at twenty-five.

When Akela scooted closer to the edge of the table and guided my dick toward her wonderful heat, I didn't think twice. I shifted her body back, angled her hips up, and pushed in. It was unlike anything I'd imagined before, only problem was my mate was a virgin too. Akela hissed out painfully. "Oh, shit." I stilled. "Sorry."

She shook her head. "No, keep going."

I reduced my pace to agonizing slowness, kissing her neck, and rubbing my thumb over her clit until she relaxed and let me in all the way. My sigh, once I was fully sheathed, was a mixture of relief and ecstasy. Not only did my girl feel unbelievable on the outside, but our mate bond twisted us tighter together and pulsed. It was like an out-of-body experience. My pleasure fed into her, erasing her discomfort, and bringing her close to orgasming. That feeling bounced back into me, until I could no longer decipher which one of us was experiencing what.

"Fuck," she breathed out, thighs clenching around my hips as her entire body shuddered. Watching her was the most erotic thing ever. It had me shooting out cum before I was ready. I wanted to live in this moment forever.

"Come home with me," I whispered unable to speak yet.

She sat up, dislodging me from where we were still joined. "I need a towel or a napkin," her voice had a quiet sad tinge that I didn't like hearing.

I pulled my pants back on and grabbed a dinner napkin from a clean stack lying on another table. When I returned, her demeanor changed. Dread settled in my stomach. "Did I hurt you?"

"Only a little," she huffed. "I gotta go."

"Akela." I helped her straighten up and get down from the table. "Don't run from this."

"You and me just don't work, Miles."

"The hell we don't!" I growled.

"Look, this was bound to happen sooner or later. The sex was great. Better than I'd expected, but this is all there can ever be between us." Her eyes watered while she fixed her hair.

"Why?" I pleaded.

"Because you are you, and I am me." She shrugged laughing brokenly. "We can't be together, it will hurt too much." With that parting shot she immediately sprinted from the room.

I stayed in the empty room, paralyzed, until the ache in my chest retuned full force. Akela had left the club and was moving away from me fast. The stronger bond was an even larger burden now that my connection to her was heightened. Perhaps a shit-ton of alcohol might dull it?

"Fuck me."

Chapter Ten

Present Day

The football game went into double overtime. It was close to ten and the almost full moon hung heavy in the sky. Kyle was the best at game day munchies. The combo pack of nurturing omega coupled with an always hungry stoner boy, meant he spent at least a third of every day in the kitchen feeding the pack. I loved watching Akela moan in appreciation over his spicy buffalo-chicken dip. Our favorite food choices had always been eerily similar. She even opted to choose the beer I bought over others in the fridge. She'd hate it if I called it out, but I know she noticed our heaping snack plates were near to identical.

Considering it had been forty hours since I slept last, I was surprisingly spry. I guess pulling off a successful kidnapping and hostage swap was an effective stimulant. The thought of taking Akela to bed was better than a five-hour energy drink.

Caius jumped up knocking the popcorn all over the floor. "Yes! Victory!"

I was barely watching the game. I was way more focused on watching my girl watching the game. I didn't give a crap who won, just glad it was over. I yawned putting on a good show. "I'm beat. Luke and Able, I want you to come with us in the morning and show Akela the forest."

"Yes, Alpha," they spoke in unison. I almost snorted and told them to knock it off but thought better. I needed Akela to see we were a pack and had a hierarchy. I wanted her to respect and admire what we'd made.

While my Viking goddess was tall compared to humans, I loved how small and dainty she felt to me. I jumped up with her cradled in my arms. She startled and clutched my shoulders. Brows driving inward to administer what I'm sure was a tongue lashing as I ran with her from the room. "Night, guys!" I shouted.

Their laughter at my antics drowned out Akela hissing at me to put her down. I had no intentions of doing so until I had her safely locked away in my room.

"Miles! For heaven's sake." She pinched my bicep hard enough to leave a bruise, then followed it up with a hard slap to my chest.

I barely registered the pain. They were love taps compared to what my older brothers used to do. The cabin wasn't massive, three bedrooms total. We were planning to add on as our pack grew. It would be more meaningful to do it now that Akela joined us. New Alpha pairing was usually followed by kids, so we would need more space. My master bedroom, though, was fairly large. I let my mate regain her feet while I locked the heavy oak door behind me.

Akela shoved her hands in her back pockets while she glowered at the king-size bed. "Where do y'all sleep while you're here?"

"Dex and Luke share a room. Able, Xan, and Caius take the other one. No one can be around Caius for too long, though, before he rubs them wrong and there's a fight, so he usually ends up on the couch. Kyle fixed up the attic for himself since he stays here year-round."

"Thought you said you had eight in your pack?" She stopped fixating on the bed and glanced back at me. "Who's the eighth?"

I put a finger through her front belt loop and tugged her into me. "I'm looking at our eighth pack member." The little pulse in the side of her neck fascinated me. It was my Akela's mood detector. Strong emotion caused it, meaning she was either about to rip me a new one or wanted me to kiss her.

I smashed my mouth against hers and when her lips parted for mine, all the tension left my shoulders. I'd wondered all day if this evening was going to end with fucking or fighting. Akela and I only did one or the other. I cradled the back of her head with my hand, my fingers pushing against her scalp. Those ocean blues met mine and a wave of tender feelings erupted out of me.

"I will never get tired of kissing you."

"Chemistry isn't one of our many problems." She bit her lip as contemplation blanketed the lust I'd just seen there.

"Oh, no, you don't." I nudged her close enough to the bed until she sat down. I grabbed an ankle and started taking off her canvas sneakers. "Stop trying to think of all the reasons you shouldn't be here right now. I know you are as badly in need of a fix as I am. You agreed to stop running from me."

She didn't fuss when I grabbed the other ankle to remove her shoe. Normally when I told her to stop running, she bolted fast. "I'm here, aren't I?" she snarled.

I really liked seeing her in my bed. "You are," I replied huskily. I toed off my shoes and huddled beside her, hands skating over any exposed flesh I could find. She always talked less about things I didn't want to hear when I was touching her.

A beautiful pink flush crept up her cheeks—she was turned on. Yet at the same time she started to stiffen. "Though I'm not sure if I should be here."

"Ha," I huffed. "That's why I had to make it so it wasn't a choice. For years I'd hoped you would just want me. I know you got the short end of the deal being mated to me. I wanted you to see me as more than the pack I came from. I wanted you to obsess about me as much as I obsessed about you." The words poured out of me surprisingly easy. Having her here only two days from the full moon made this almost a sure thing. If our wolves changed together, our mate bond would snap permanently in place allowing for the pack bonds to form. Our wolf side didn't care about our hangups or our baggage. It would simply recognize its mate. "Now, I'll settle for the scraps. Having some of you is infinitely better than having none of you."

She rested her palm against my cheek. Her eyes pooled with unshed tears while she leaned forward and administered the sweetest, softest kiss I'd ever been granted. An intense emotion shook me. I could feel our mate bond, usually a sluggish passive thing, start to pulse in a rhythm that matched my pounding heart.

I completely and utterly froze, terrified that no matter what I did next, it would push her away. She pulled back to view my face, clearly puzzled. "What's wrong?"

A shaky breath escaped my lips. Before I could stop myself and act more like an alpha, I did the most omega thing ever and talked about my insecurities. "I'm scared shitless I'm going to mess this up. There's nothing in this damn world I want more than you, but nothing I've done so far has proven my worth to you as your mate." The silence stretched between us and the word vomitorium wouldn't stop. "I lost my shit seeing you on Alpha Austin's porch, arms crossed over your chest and looking at me like I was dirt. Every one there celebrating the kidnapping of Raff's mate. A total Grey wolf thing to do, by the way. I was like, shit, well, if it worked for him, why the fuck not? And then you're here and my brain is telling me, wow, that shit worked. Yet my heart is telling me not to hope. So instead, I'm begging for scraps and wondering if that makes me a weak alpha, like my father. I just…"

My rambling was cut off by Akela jumping on me. Her mouth latched onto mine and she sucked on my bottom lip almost to the point of pain. Her hands tunneled under my shirt, nails marking my back. She grinded against me, making these devilish little moans that had my balls tightening.

The word mush circling my mind went blissfully silent. These signals I understood clearly. My mate wanted me. Yet, the last time we were together, I'd thrown down an ultimatum. I had to stick to it. I pinned her down on the bed by laying my body on top of hers. She took the movement as encouragement and sucked on my tongue with renewed vigor. It took all the strength I had to break away from her kiss and rest my weight on my forearms. She nibbled on her bottom lip while her eyes searched mine. The heat radiating from her core made my dick twitch in anticipation. Her hips rose off the bed while her greedy clit sought out the friction of my cock trapped in my jeans. It was close to my undoing.

"Say it," I demanded.

I was grateful she didn't act confused or tighten her lips stubbornly. A tilted smile graced her mouth and a guilty little chuckle accompanied it. It was like she'd hoped I wouldn't have asked, but knew that expectation was futile.

"It's real," she whispered.

"Nope." I shook my head, our faces so close that our noses rubbed. "The whole thing."

"Why do you want it so badly? You know the truth." Her stubborn side was showing.

"Because you've rejected me enough. This has meaning."

"All right, Miles, I understand." She took in a deep breath and looked at me solemnly. "You are my true mate. What we have between us is real."

I couldn't think of a single dirty thing ever spoken to me that was sexier than that. My hand slid inside her stretchy leggings, cupping her sex, and using the heel of my palm to grind her clit while my fingers explored how incredibly wet her little thong was. She wiggled under me, delighted by my touch. Her own hands were deftly unbuttoning my fly and freeing me. I sprang out fully erect and grunted as her hand circled around my shaft and squeezed. We probably could have gotten off in about a minute flat, like two horny teenagers hoping not to get caught by the parents down the hall. It had been too long since we'd been together and there was no way I wasn't going to come inside her.

"I want you naked." I rolled over onto my knees while yanking off her skintight leggings.

Her throaty chuckle had my spine tingling. "You're sure a demanding one tonight."

"I reckon it's something you'll get used to." I pulled my shirt over my head and divested myself of the jeans.

"Well," she replied breathlessly. She paused looking up at me before slowly removing one bra strap then the next. Stopping right before her breast would be exposed, she gave me a cocky smirk. "Don't get used to me easily taking orders." She dropped the bra and my mouth went dry. She was crazy beautiful, so fucking sexy it was hard to think.

"Baby, are you calling a double abduction scheme with a hideaway in the woods, after a thirteen-year game of cat-and-mouse easy?"

She rolled her eyes. "You better put that thing inside of me and make me come. Unless of course you changed your mind?"

I stalked her, then. Working my way up her body starting at her ankles. Switching between kisses, licks, and gentle nips until I reached her folds. I peered up and she was looking down at me, eyes glassy with desire. "I will never change my mind about you." I kissed her softly a few times before sucking her almost roughly into my mouth the way I knew she liked it. It had been ages since I'd been inside her, but when it came to Akela, I was an expert. She always climaxed quickly this way and tonight was no exception. Before the throbbing of her first orgasm abated, I was balls-deep, lifting her hips for the best angle and sinking in. She was tight. I had to grit my teeth and slow down to make it last. She was convulsing around me and I knew if I timed it right I could get her to chase one orgasm directly after the next. My thumb grazed her clit and her thighs flexed tight around mine. Her ankles were hooked together pressing against the small of my back as she brought her hips up to meet me thrust for thrust. I clenched my teeth to hold on.

I'd gone too damn long without this woman, without the other half of my soul. The mate bond flared with heat. I felt its caress down my spine, on the sides of my torso, and around my neck. It grew in intensity bouncing back from me to her as the pleasure mounted. Akela's back arched off the bed, thighs rigid bands around me. Her moan caused beads of sweat to form on my brow. I waited for the telltale signs of her second orgasm to start. When the fluttering finally began and she clamped down around me, I cried out, a mixture of relief and intense release. My entire body shuddered as waves of pleasure crested and crashed over us both.

I turned our bodies with her on top of my chest, too afraid that in my exhaustion I would crush her. I'd been living on pure adrenaline these last two days. My climax, like a shot of morphine, dulled my pain and made it hard to keep my eyes open. She nibbled and sucked on my pecks, riding me till we were both too sensitive to move. With her warm body plastered against mine and the bond thrumming in time with our heartbeats, I let sleep finally wash over me.

Chapter Eleven

Present Day

Morning sunlight played on my eyelids causing me to bury my face in the pillow. I could feel a tugging, not on my physical body but on our bond. My mate needed something. I hoped it was more of what we did last night. Cracking open an eye I peered at her. Seeing her in my bed in the full light of day was a dream I often had but never thought would come true. She was lying on her side, her top leg bare and out of the covers, her hands in prayer position sandwiched between her pillow and her cheek. I got the sense she had been watching me for a while.

"Morning," my voice was rough from sleep.

"You sleep like the dead," she griped.

I scooted closer to her. Resting my hand on her hip, I buried my nose in her coconut-scented hair. "What is it you need, baby?"

Her reply was a grumble. "Everything."

I lightly brushed my lips over her earlobe. She arched into me, shivering delicately. I loved her reaction to my touch. "Where should I start?"

She roughly shoved me away. Sitting up, she tugged at the blankets covering her perfect breasts. "I'm serious. I need everything," she pouted. "Your abduction and ransom scheme didn't leave much time for getting any of my things. I have a backpack with my wallet, a makeup bag, one change of clothes, and a bottle of Advil. I don't even have any clean underwear or a damn toothbrush."

I scrubbed my face trying to get more fully awake. "I promise we'll pick up your things after the shift. In the meantime, I have a new toothbrush in the bathroom, a hairbrush, and that shampoo and conditioner you like."

"And I am, what? Supposed to walk around nude?" she sassed. Before my grin could split my face in half at the suggestion, she held up her hand. "Strike that. No need to answer."

I couldn't resist wiggling my eyebrows before I conceded. "There are a few clothes in the closet that will fit you. While I would love a naked Akela 24/7, I don't think I'd love to see the guys enjoying the view of what's mine."

She answered with an eye roll and quickly hopped up to examine the closet. The former alpha of the house could not look at his wife's things after she died. There was a ton of stuff I'd sorted. Some things I thought Tom would want to have again one day, those I packed in a rubber bin and stored in the basement. I also gave a bunch of stuff to charity. There were a few things, though, that made me think of Akela. I kept those. Not because I thought she would ever actually use them, but because it made pretending this day would come possible.

She stood in front of the closet for over ten minutes examining the items. They were not new. So she would know I didn't buy them for her. I wasn't well off like her former pack. Austin's lab had tons of money. I was a car mechanic. I wondered what her reaction would be. Would she find me incredibly pathetic or weird if I told her the truth?

She pulled out a tie-dyed oversized tee and a pair of fleece joggers. Turning to me with her head tilted to the side, she asked the question I was wondering how to answer. "Whose clothes are these in your closet?"

Akela was my mate, it's almost physically impossible for our kind to be with another once the mate bond sparks. "Why? Are you jealous?" I teased.

She shrugged and pulled on the tee. I was happy to see her forego a bra. "Not really. I figured given the nature of our relationship other companionship would be needed."

If I hadn't still been laying down, I might have fallen over. "What are you saying?"

She pulled on the pants acting all nonchalant. "It's just that we've had some really long dry spells. People still have needs."

My temperature skyrocketed as I sat up. "What the fuck are you saying?"

Her eyebrows jumped past her hairline. "Why are you yelling at me?"

She was lucky I wasn't shaking the shit out of her. "Are you implying that you expected me, your mate, to cheat on you? Or are you saying…" The thought of Akela with another man made me sick. I couldn't even say it aloud. She'd always been different than other mates. Rejecting me constantly, even though at times I thought our connection was solid.

"Oh, calm down. Jeez, Miles. It's human nature to fill the void."

I tossed the covers back, jumped out of bed, and went toe to toe with her. "We are not human!" I shouted, my nose inches from her own.

I watched her hands curl into fists, her long nails biting into skin. She had no intention of backing down from my rage. "What is your fucking problem?" she hissed.

"For the last seven years? *You*!" I was shaking. Outrage vibrated through my entire body.

Her eyes narrowed to slits. "Then let me go. I will get out of your life."

An ugly laugh escaped. "You'd like that,

wouldn't you? Never giving me anything. Only ever taking from me. Your constant running from what we are to each other *is* my problem. I'm your true mate. We have a bond. Leaving me just rips my soul in two. Hearing that you so casually have fucked other men, while I can't even go near another woman without my stomach curdling, is killing me." My anger deflated leaving despair to fill the void. I sank back down on the edge of the bed. "I know you'll never love me like you do your birth pack. I'd just hoped, stupidly yet again, that we would be forming our own pack."

Akela shivered and hugged herself. Tears pooled in her eyes as she looked everywhere around the room but at me. "I've never been with anyone else, Miles." Her tone was soft. "Seeing another woman's clothes hanging next to yours was a bit of a shock." She looked up and blew out a large breath trying to stop the tears from flowing. My girl hardly showed a soft side and I perked up at her announcement. "I have pushed you away, time and time again. How could I have the right to be angry if you needed more and found it with someone else?" She dragged the heel of her hand under each eye and sucked in her lips. She was beautiful even when she cried.

"Babe," I calmed down. "You know how mates work. It's pretty much you or bust. Tom left all his wife's things here. I kept some things I thought you'd like. She had nice things. Things I can't afford to buy you."

She sighed and sat beside me. "But you did buy the shampoo I like?"

I wish I could peek into that brain of hers and know for just a minute what she was thinking. I've never met a puzzle quite like her. "I always loved that you smell like a tropical vacation. Your coconut oil shampoo is one of the few luxuries I can splurge for."

She turned to me, her eyes tracing over my

features. A single tear made its way down her cheek while she stared. Her lips twisted in a sad smile. "What about my toothpaste? Did you buy the brand I use?"

I nodded.

She leaned in and kissed me softly on top of my shoulder before standing. "Thanks. I think I'll take a shower, then."

I watched her walk away. I wanted nothing more than to go after her and hold her tight. *Baby steps*, I reminded myself. She didn't run. She spent the night. She's still here. It's the most progress we've made in years.

****

"Shit, man! I know your pops was always whipped by your momma, but I didn't think that was the kind of alpha you would be." Dex was lying in wait in the hallway, ambushing me as I made my way to the kitchen.

"What are you going on about?" I would generally have stopped in my tracks and asserted dominance over a pack mate's condescending tone, but I didn't want Akela to hear. Whatever stupid ass shit was about to leave Dex's mouth needed to be well out of her hearing range. I strode down the hallway and passed the living room toward the door. Dex was slow to follow or answer my question.

Reaching the cabin door with knob in hand, I turned to glare at him. "Outside. Now!"

That got him to pick up speed, yet the attitude still hung heavy on him. He reached back and slammed the door once he was outside. "What? The princess can't be disturbed?"

My hands curled into fists as white-hot rage settled in my stomach. It had been at least two years since I'd bloodied my knuckles on Dex's face. I'd hoped we would be past his tantrums. "What's your problem?"

"My problem?" he asked incredulously. "What's *your* problem? You have a strong massive pack just waiting for you to claim it. Instead, we are out here in this run-down cabin playing house with a fucking Red."

"Damn it, Dex. You love our old pack so much, why don't you go back to it, eh? That woman in there is my true mate. Only with her can I be alpha of any pack."

"That's not entirely true, plenty of alpha make bonds with alpha females not their true mates. You could have your pick, man. It doesn't have to be this one." Dex grimaced as he pointed back at the door with his thumb.

"That's only because they never found their true mate, Dex. Trust me on this, once you do your wolf will not accept another. So, if you have a problem with any of this, get out. Get out now. Because I do *not* want to hear the same tired whining come out of your mouth." My words were close to a growl as they escaped from clenched teeth.

I was finding it hard to stay calm. With the full moon just a day away, our bodies prepared for the change, causing a riot of emotions. A group of males without an alpha female often pounded on each other to let off steam, but that wasn't me. I only fought by necessity. I would never become my brothers, or worse, my mother. I watched as Dex realized I wouldn't demand his submission. Saw that he thought less of me for it too.

"I keep waiting for the punch line, Miles. I can't make sense of you. I thought we had a plan? We talked about it when I left the old pack. I've been patient, but it's been ten years, man! You say she's the one. Fine, she's the one. Then let's make plans after the change comes to head back! We take our current pack and merge with our old pack. We would be massive! A force for other packs to reckon with. You gotta think bigger than what we have now." Dex threw his hands up in the air with frustrated disdain.

"No, Dex. You talked about a plan and I listened to you talk. I haven't then or now *ever* wanted that. This pack is just beginning. It could be anything we want to make it. Other mates for you all, kids, a *real* family, one where it isn't our daily goal to bruise and wound our pack mates. When I left home, it was for good. This fantasy you carry around sounds like a nightmare to me."

The passionate fire dimmed behind Dex's eyes. He gnashed his teeth while shaking his head. "This is bullshit." He turned on his heel and stormed off, putting on one hell of an act, as if my words were the ultimate betrayal. I've told him countless times over the years the same thing. I hoped this time it finally sunk in.

Chapter Twelve

Present Day

I grumbled to myself during my shower, still pissed at Dex's outburst. After all these years together, I felt more than a sense of obligation for him. He was my first pack mate, but it bothered me how he spurned Akela from the get-go. Getting that woman to warm up to me was difficult enough without him constantly throwing shade. Toweling off, I chucked the cloth harder than necessary and knocked the hamper on its side. I'm usually a true clean freak and would have immediately put the thing back in its place, but I was distracted.

The shower was the first time I'd truly let Akela out of my sight, I worried how my pack of miscreants would be with her when I wasn't around. She deserved better than me, I knew that, yet fate had made the choice for both of us. I suffered for years due to her indifference, and she would most likely be miserable lowering her standards to accept this pack. No matter how many times life told me otherwise, I still held a shred of hope that we could create a home. I'd never experienced that sense of belonging. I needed my mate to make this constant burn in my chest go away. I wanted her to finally want me.

I looked at the rumpled sheets on the bed and wished I could have slept another five hours. I'd been depriving myself of sleep from the moment I saw Raff's newly claimed alpha female standing next to my mate on the porch of Alpha Austin's house. Chloe was just a means to an end in all this. Just a tool for me to get Akela to take my claim seriously, but it was personal too.

Seeing Akela next to her, both their arms crossed, looking down their noses at me, made me see red. I could never hurt my mate, but I did feel vindication in messing with Raff's woman. After all, it was his father's pack that decided, on the whole, I was scum.

I snagged a pair of sweatpants to wear and nothing else. After making sure the pack was settled in, I had high hopes of coming back here this afternoon and crashing a bit longer, hopefully with Akela snuggled at my side. As I opened the door the sweet sound of feminine laughter carried down the hallway. I could hear deeper voices answering back, and quickened my pace to the kitchen.

The sight of Akela made me hold my breath. She was bending down, oven mittens on, and taking out what looked like monkey bread. The strong smell of sugary cinnamon confirmed my guess. Kyle and Xan moved over so she could set it down on the counter. My girl noticed me as she was removing her mitts. Her eyes twinkled when she looked at me. I had to remind myself for a second time to exhale.

"Perfect!" she trilled. "You got here just in time to try my momma's recipe. It won her a bake-off five years ago. I was pleasantly surprised when I saw how well-stocked Kyle keeps the pantry." She smiled sweetly at the omega and he blushed from his cheeks down to his neck. "I was sure we would be eating beans out of a can for the next day."

"You baked for us, babe?" I couldn't be more pleased, it was a good sign. I walked to the other side of the kitchen island across from them.

"I'm not going to lie, Miles," Kyle slid the plate farther away from me. "I think it would be better if you didn't eat this."

Did she put laxatives in it? Or poison? Is that why

she was in here laughing? Was she planning on incapacitating me and slipping away? My gut clenched at the implications.

"Because I know," Kyle continued. "I'll never get any once you start." Kyle then stuffed a large bite into his mouth.

My eyes practically bug out of my head. Omegas never ate before their alphas.

Both Akela and Xan start busting up. "I can't believe you actually did it!" she exclaimed while brushing tears from her eyes.

"I didn't think you had it in you, brother!" Xan slaps him on the back and I note that Kyle was a little green while waiting on my reaction.

"She asked me to do that," Kyle blurted, while quickly shooting guilty puppy-dog eyes at my mate begging her forgiveness for selling her out.

Seeing Akela's dazzling smile stopped any harsh words that might have left my mouth. Kyle did it for her. He went against all his natural instincts to make her happy. It restored my faith in omegas. There was a reason they were always the alpha female's favorite. I should have brought Kyle instead of Dex with me the day I boldly drove up to her pack's front door. I might have had a completely different reception.

Akela tore off a piece of the bread heavily doused in cinnamon and sugar and brought it up to my lips. "Wanna taste?" she practically purred, totally content to wrap my entire pack around her little finger. The joke was on her, though. It's what we wanted.

I grabbed her wrist holding it in place while I accepted her offering then proceeded to lick the sticky goodness off her fingers. Slowly sucking each digit and swirling my tongue over her prints. Her pupils dilated, growing large and dropping to drink in my bare chest. I watched her pink tongue skate over her top lip. It looked like my girl might want to devour me as well.

"I'll just put on another pot of coffee," Kyle said and backed away from us.

"I'll grab plates," Xan spoke almost at the same time.

Akela laughed as the guys made tracks, not showing a hint of embarrassment about our PDA. Our mate bond did a little dance. I strained my senses to see if I could feel the beginning of a pack bond. Was she accepting them this soon?

"I think I'll wash my hands before I eat." She winked playfully at me. Her index finger brushed over my lips before she turned to the sink.

She even made turning the water on a turn-on. I regretted not taking the opportunity to shower with her earlier. The idea of beads of water dripping down her flawless skin made me thirsty.

A deep masculine moan interrupted my thoughts in the opposite of sexy way. "Oh, God, what is that wonderful smell?" Caius stumbled from his room, eyes closed in a moment of bliss.

"Dude! Put on some clothes!" Xan covered his eyes and fake gagged.

Caius looked down like he had not even considered his current state.

"Are you wearing a woman's thong?" I asked incredulously. Boxer briefs at breakfast is acceptable, but this sheer red contraption was smaller than a banana hammock and not what I wanted to see first thing in the morning,

"Oh, shit!" Caius laughed but made no attempt to change. The cocky bastard walked even further into the kitchen in search of the baked goods that permeated the air. "I went to visit the ranger last night to make sure we're in the clear for the change. Didn't get home till early this morning. These are hers." He wiggled his eyebrows at Xan who was using an extended hand to block out the site of Caius's barely concealed package.

"Classy," was Aklea's snarky response. "But if you want to eat, go grab some shorts, Romeo. I only do naked groups after a change."

"Duly noted, Alpha." Caius saluted her and sauntered back to his room. A tiny red string his only coverage from behind. "*Wake up, kid*!" he shouted at the top of his lungs probably scaring the crap out of poor Able, his other roommate. "Mommy made us breakfast and you gotta clean up to eat."

His sarcastic tone wasn't lost on me. The urge to hit him on the side of the head was strong. Couldn't he at least try to make a good impression? The change was tomorrow night! Could we just hold our shit together until then? Please!

Akela slid a plate down the island. It stopped right in front of me. "Eat up, Daddy." The smirk on her face let me know she was just going with it.

I fucking loved this woman.

Chapter Thirteen

Three Years Ago

Akela: **Crescent Moon Motel, Athens, Georgia, Friday, 8 pm**

Miles: **That's over a five-hour drive.**

Akela: **But this motel is so fitting, don't you think?**

Miles: **How about my place?**

Akela: **You can have me for the entire weekend … at the motel**

Miles: **I'll see you Friday.**

I stared at my phone wishing Akela didn't have such power over me. We fought last week when I started pushing back on these "out-of-town" random hookup spots. She teased me, asking where my sense of adventure was. I know the truth, though. She doesn't want to get caught being with me. She doesn't want to acknowledge what we have. She's ashamed of it. The damn thing is, I can't live without her. As soon as our mate bond snapped in place, I got physically ill when I was away from her too long. I know it's the same for her. These little hookups used to be only once a month, but now they're almost weekly.

She never offered a weekend before. In the last four years, I've only gotten her to fall asleep in my arms twice and both times after a night of heavy drinking.

Luke, a lone wolf that blew into town a year ago and decided for some crazy reason to stick around and join my pack, passed me a beer. He glanced at my screen before taking the barstool next to me. I'd imagine humans would see it as an invasion of privacy, but shifters are made different. We crave open community. Without real pack bonds where we can sense each other, it is common to overstep and not allow others privacy. Even as the alpha, I tolerate liberties.

"Your girl still making you work for it?" If that line had come from Dex it would have been a jab. Another fight about how she wasn't worth it. Like it was a choice I made. Luke, however, looked concerned.

"Yeah." I took a long thoughtful sip. "Never offered up a full weekend before. Never been more than one night."

Luke's solemn expression visibly brightened. "That's a great sign."

"How you figure?" I scoffed.

"She's been ramping up these meetings and now extending the time. She must be getting close to accepting the bond."

As stupid as it would be to hope, Luke's words lightened my mood considerably. "I'm from a pack she and her entire family despises. She keeps me a secret from them. She will never accept me, man."

"That's not the way I see it. She hasn't met your pack yet. Not the pack you plan to have."

I looked at him totally lost. "What are you talking about?"

Luke looked around the bar keeping his voice low. His actions were uncertain and strangely shy. "Dex is always talking about your plans on taking out your dad and claiming that pack. I've gotten to know you over the months, and I don't see you doing it. Caius is a complete no-filter jerk most of the time, but you gave the dude a job when he was down on his luck and he secretly worships you. Able is seriously a compulsive thief, would take these barstools with him tonight if they were not bolted to the floor. For you, he straightens up his act and does the right thing when you ask. Xan was not a huge fan of the South, but he sticks it out because he sees you as his alpha. I thought I'd be a lone wolf the rest of my life after losing my family, but around you that loss is slightly dulled. We're your pack. Akela sees you with a few of us occasionally, but you haven't introduced us or explained who we are to you and one day to her."

Luke was a guy of few words, but I do believe he just proposed. The idea of presenting my pack had merit. It would make my claim on Akela more substantial than just a mate bond. She was an alpha too, and an alpha was best with a pack. "Saying we're a pack and acting like a pack are two different things. We hardly have our shit together."

The arctic wolf shifter appeared thoughtful. "You think she'll reject us?"

"She hasn't exactly warmed up to me, and I've known she was my mate for ten years now." I could hear the bitterness in my voice. I felt strangled by our circumstances. "She watched me snub my brother and distance myself from him and will never forgive me. She thinks being with me is a betrayal to Tate."

Taking a slow sip of his beer, his light-blond brows crinkled as he thought. "Then the only thing to do is set it right." He held up four fingers in front of him and ticked them off with each sentence. "Make peace with your brother. Take Tom up on his offer to give our pack his old cabin. Fix the place up so it feels like the permanent home a pack needs to have. One of these weekends get her out there and we'll join you, convince her it's better to become a pack than to be a lone wolf. She can't stay an alpha in another pack forever."

"You think it's that simple, heh?" I frowned.

"It's not foolproof," he said and shrugged. "I'll admit. What you really need is to find an omega looking for a pack. That would seal the deal for sure!"

"An omega," I choked on my beer. "What the hell

for?"

"Please! Omegas are like little puppies to alpha females. They instantly fall for them." Luke laughed.

"I'd like to get her to fall for me first," I grumbled.

The sound of shattered glass interrupted Luke's reply. We both jumped up and headed outside to find out what caused the noise. I expected to find kids throwing rocks or maybe a car thief. What I got was a family reunion.

My eyes first landed on Dex standing off to the side looking a bit smug, but once he saw me in the doorway, a sense of unease wrapped around him and his eyes lowered with guilt. My two older brothers were here in the flesh, beating the crap out of some poor sap. A smashed-in bloodied car window made my jaw tick. The site of a prone body lying in the gutter made my stomach turn. It was Tate. Seems like brother dears used our baby bro as a battering ram.

"What the actual fuck!" I roared. Both my brothers might have had an inch on me and a few more pounds of muscle, but I was the only alpha in this parking lot. They both froze as I made my way over to check on Tate. I gently rolled him over. There was a gash on his forehead where he must have hit the window and another lump on the back of his head. It looked like he was hit from behind with a heavy object. His face and hair were covered in blood. I tore off my tee, the only thing I had to use to stop the bleeding. "You assholes! Are you trying to kill him?"

My oldest brother chuckled. "It would be a kindness. Something we were meant to do a long time ago. World don't need the runts of the litter anyway."

"What the world doesn't need, Scott, is brain-dead morons like you in it." He attempted to stare me down, but I put every ounce of dominance I had into my glare. Scott lasted a few seconds before he looked away. I shifted my glare over to Dex. "Did you enjoy the show?"

Dex looked more contrite than I'd ever seen him before. "Alpha..." He swallowed loudly, his eyeline never leaving my shoes. "It was just a bit of fun at first that got out of hand."

"Come on, Miles," my other brother jeered. "Dex invited us out tonight. We were coming to join you and passed these two going at it like horny teens in the alley. We were only busting his chops about it. It was Tate that got a little hotheaded and started shouting at us. Well, that couldn't go unpunished. You know our ways."

I peered closer at the other man on the ground at exactly the moment Tate started to come to. He winced and cradled his head in his hands. "Easy there, little bro. You took more than one lump."

"Get your hands off me," he ground out through clenched teeth. He was clearly in a daze as he shoved away from me and attempted to crawl toward our brother's other victim. "Get away from him," he slurred.

Luke had gone over to try to help the other guy. He scrunched his brows in concern. "He's pretty fucked up." He looked at me. "He needs medical attention."

I wanted to bash my older brothers' heads in but I had to calm down and focus on making this right. "I'll bring my truck around. We can take him to the shop." Shifters didn't go to normal hospitals for obvious reasons.

"I think we better call an ambulance." Luke held his cell in his hand waiting for my confirmation.

"Shit," I swore. "He's human?"

"Get away from him!" Tate was still unsteady. His eyes glazed and wild and he finally reached the guy.

"No, no, no, no," he moaned repeatedly.

"Jeez, Scott! We don't beat up humans. Ever! They aren't as resilient as us and it comes with more heat and scrutiny than Wa'ya need.

Scott looked at Tate with disgust. "Everything about him is weak. Austin raised a bunch of pansies."

My hard-fought calm evaporated instantly. I saw red. The next thing I knew, my hands were around my eldest brother's throat and I was choking the life out of him. My other brother jumped on my back. Luke leaped over the human to come to my aid. A car screeched to a stop behind us. Dex attempted to step in but tripped over Tate and landed on his legs. Other patrons of the bar started streaming outside, and I could hear sirens in the distance. Things were not going well.

The distinct sound of a shotgun being caulked was followed by an enraged female voice. "Hey dickheads!" Akela stood over us pointing a sawed-off in our direction. Dex raised his hands while rolling off Tate. I released Scott's neck and threw my other brother from my back. A storm was raging in Akela's eyes as she took in the entire scene. She was glorious in her wrath. She pointed the shotgun directly at Luke. "You. Put Tate in my car."

"But Jason," Tate protested as Luke pulled him up from his armpits.

"Sorry, Tate." She grimaced looking behind her. The lights of the cop cars could be seen in the distance. "Help will be here for him sooner if we leave him, longer if we take him."

Luke awkwardly stuffed my little brother into the car that Akela parked directly behind our brawl. He struggled to get back out. "Can't leave him with them."

"It will be fine." She said soothingly before turning around and breathing fire. "These losers will scatter the second we leave." Her eyes were glued to me as she spoke. "Control your dogs!"

I knew things were bad. Tate covered in blood. Me, shirtless and fighting in the street. It was her look of absolute disdain, however, that made me want to panic. She thought I was an accomplice in this beating and not the one to put a stop to it. There was no time to set things right. She jumped in the car and tore out of the parking lot as the police started to pull in.

"Gotta go, Miles!" Luke yelled, still waiting for me, though, before fleeing.

I nodded and started running in the opposite direction of the sirens, leaving that poor man bleeding on the sidewalk and my mate thinking I was the guilty party.

Fuck my life.

****

Months had passed since the night Tate was beaten by our older brothers, and Akela continued to refuse to see me. It had me on edge all the time. I've gone off and wailed on Dex for even mentioning her name and shoved Caius against a wall for challenging me about what color to paint the inside of our new cabin. I know it's my wolf freaking out about our mate, but there isn't a fucking thing I can do about it. I can't storm up to her house in the heart of Austin's pack. It wouldn't end well. I'd end up hurting someone she loves if they tried to stop me, and she'd never forgive me.

The only solution when my beast was driving me to track her down, was to drown him out with as much alcohol as I could swallow. Hungover from the night before, I was still desperate to suppress my urges. Luckily, Able agreed to drive me to the liquor store. I felt like absolute shit and had no desire to be in a social setting like a bar. The plan for the night was a large bottle of whiskey and my couch.

Able parked his new Toyota Corolla in the parking lot and looked over at me. "Hey, Boss, you want to wait here?"

I eyed him warily, afraid if I said yes, he'd just go in and shoplift. Able's not one willing to pay for things. "Nah." I grimaced as I open the door. "I might grab some snacks too. Not sure what I want."

Lumbering at a snail's pace, I entered the store with my pack mate trailing behind me. My head was pounding and a complete fog enveloped my senses. I made a beeline to the bottles of the hard stuff and pulled one from the shelf without ever noticing the other customer squatting down grabbing an item from the bottom section. I stepped right on her hand.

"Motherfucker," she cussed sucking in a pain-filled gasp.

The murkiness around me evaporated instantly. The string constricting my heart unraveled. I could breathe in deeply. I bent down and hoisted Akela up by her elbow. An electric current of pure pleasure shot up my arm from the brief touch. "Are you all right?" my voice sounded gruff and ill-used. "I didn't see you there."

"Let go." She rotated out of my grip but stumbled. I caught her before she faceplanted directly into a stacked display of Southern Comfort. Sensing she was unsteady on her feet, I pulled her further into the aisle. Taking advantage of the rescue, I couldn't resist circling both arms around her waist. Sure looked like she'd been starting early on the same hair-of-the-dog remedy I was working diligently on. Her hair was a greasy tangle tied up at the top of her head. She was wearing a threadworn concert tee stained by either barbeque sauce or blood. An oversized flannel shirt missing every button on the front but two hung limply from her shoulders but luckily trailed down to cover her ass, since I wondered if the skirt she had on was just a tube top substituting for a bottom. The entire outfit was finished off by mismatched flip-flops. My girl was a hot mess.

"You are one stubborn woman," I grumbled.

"I'm not talking to you," she ground out through clenched teeth.

"This has gone on long enough," I shot back firmly. It was one thing to make me miserable, but I was not going to let her self-destruct as well. Ignoring her protests and curses, I shuffled her out the side door and into the alleyway behind the store. The skunky smell of stale beer wafting from the large green dumpster wasn't the most romantic location to make amends, but it would have to do.

Before I could lay into her for not taking care of herself, I had this overwhelming need to hold her tight. I set down the bottle I accidentally took outside, wrapped my arms around her and pressed her close to my chest. Obviously showering had not been a priority for either of us, but I didn't care in the slightest. Standing here with her tucked against me was all I truly needed. The happy little thrum in my chest grew stronger the longer neither of us moved. The intensity spiked till my dick grew hard and my body vibrated with need. Akela was not impervious. She rubbed her face against my collarbone and lifted on her toes till her lips found the flesh of my neck near my ear.

Groaning, I shifted my hands under her ass and lifted her up. I needed access to her mouth. I sucked her lush bottom lip before she opened and our tongues battled. Akela circled her legs around my torso forcing me to firmly cup her ass to provide support. The motion delivered a revelation. Her ass was bare. My fingers pushed forward. Sure enough, she was panty free. The switch in my brain that provides higher levels of reasoning malfunctioned. I took three large strides till I had her pinned against the brick wall. Akela's switch obviously had stopped working earlier in the day when she dressed herself. Her hands dropped to my fly. She unbuttoned and pulled me out in what had to be a world record.

Either time froze or sped up. I have little recollection except for pounding my mate senseless between two dumpsters, in broad daylight, in the back alley of a liquor store, on a Tuesday. I did have perfect clarity the minute we both orgasmed and time and space returned to normal, and with it, the complete awkwardness of our situation.

"Fuck," I grimaced. I pulled out and looked around to make sure we had not been observed. Then, instead of apologizing, I opted to lash out. "You're not wearing any underwear? Is this scrap of fabric even a skirt?"

"Does it look like I've done laundry to you?" she seethed as I set her down.

I could have kicked myself for opening my big mouth, but it just kept spilling out. "I cannot believe you are out in public like this. It's not safe! You're dressed like a blind hooker."

"You know, Miles…" She backed away from me, pulled that ridiculously small scrap of fabric down to cover her lady bits, and scowled. "I'm the one pissed off at you. So, if this is how you want to do it, then fine! Fucking leave me alone. I can't keep doing this with you. We. Are. Over."

"You are such a child!" I shouted directly in her face. "You never play fair."

"I don't play fair?" Her eyes bulged out. "Was what you did to Tate and his friend fair?"

"I ran out to stop that fight! I never wanted to see my brother get hurt again." I pounded on my chest. The anguish the memory evoked was still raw.

A flicker of doubt crossed the ocean of blue in her eyes.

"Did Tate tell you I hurt him?" It crushed me to ask the question. My voice noticeably shook.

Tears slid down Akela's cheeks. "He doesn't remember much from the beating. He's been a shell of himself. His friend Jason, well, more than a friend..." Her breathing hitched and she gulped a sob. "He didn't survive."

"Oh, God." My stomach rolled.

"I made him leave Jason there on the street to die alone." She sobbed harder now and I pulled her to my chest again.

"You did the right thing. If you had taken him with you and he had died in your car, it would have been a lot of heat on your pack," I whispered into her hair as I rubbed her back.

She looked up at me. Her tear-stained cheeks sent millions of knives to my gut. "Promise me," she started, her lips settling into a firm line. "Promise me you had nothing to do with the beating."

I took her right hand and placed it directly over my heart. "I swear on our bond, I knew nothing about it. I heard a noise. Went outside. Immediately jumped in to put a stop to it." I stared solemnly into her eyes until I was convinced she believed me. "Can I see Tate?"

She shook her head. "He left Austin's pack last month."

"What do you mean? Where did he go?" I asked worriedly.

"Raff started a pack. Jason wasn't the love of Tate's life, but they were close and he needs distance from all of this to heal. Raff came to collect him after the last full moon. Tate looked relieved to go."

She had no idea the impact her words had on me. I was crushed. I thought Tate would leave Austin's pack one day, but only to join mine, so we could be a family again. But he didn't even consider joining me. I was only worthy of the misfits.

As if on cue Able pulled up at the end of the alley and rolled down his window. "Hey, Boss!" he shouted. "We really gotta go." He was frantically waving at me.

I turned back to Akela. "Come home with me. We can get washed up, I'll cook you dinner." She had never said yes before, but her excuse was always Tate.

Glancing over at Able's car she shook her head and any hope I had plummeted. "I need to get home."

Rejection was a bitter pill to swallow. One would think I'd be immune to it by now. "I should be your home," I said with little inflection and headed to the car.

I slid into the passenger seat and buckled up. "Why didn't you just wait in the parking lot?" I questioned with a groan as I noticed the back seat full of snacks and liquor. "Did you pay for that?"

"I paid for some of it?" was his sheepish reply. "The trick is not to just walk out without buying anything. Like you did," he countered with a pointed look. "With the whiskey."

Oh, shit! As Able peeled away I watched the owner of the shop round the corner to where I left Akela, post-coitus, presumably still pissed off, and seemingly in possession of a stolen bottle of whiskey I left by her feet. I'm pretty sure I just landed myself another few months in the doghouse.

Chapter Fourteen

Present Day

Breakfast was a pleasant affair, that is, once Caius put some pants on. Not having Dex around changed the group dynamic. Akela was noticeably more open. The six of us actually used the country oak dining room table for an honest-to-goodness sit-down family-style meal. Luke slowly sipped his coffee while a dreamy expression floated over his pale features. Able took advantage of Luke's distraction sliding bacon from the pale shifter's plate to his own, but a single frown from Akela had him hanging his head and putting it back before Luke even noticed. Xan and Caius were retelling their favorite story of when an older human woman came into the shop. Her car had been towed in and she had no clue why it wasn't working. She'd been feeding it all good stuff. Which then always prompted, "She what?" Then they regale the listener with a crazy list of the sixty-four items they extracted from inside the engine of the car.

"Wait a minute." Akela paused to take a breath and wipe her eyes, "She stuck fried frog legs in where?"

"She said she was looking for the intake manifold," Caius answered with a grin. "'Cause where else would you want to take in something?"

Akela's full belly laugh at the question stirred a fire inside my own. This felt so right. All this time. All these years. She was finally here, with me, with my pack, soon to be *our* pack. I could've been pissed that getting here was a bumpy road, requiring a prisoner exchange, but fuck it. She slept in my bed, made me breakfast, and was sitting here listening to car mechanic stories with a smile on her face. This is all I ever wanted.

"You must have made a fortune off of her," Akela chuckled.

"Sadly, no." Xan shook his head solemnly. "Our alpha barely charged her enough to cover the cost of the parts. Said it wouldn't be fair."

Akela shot a questioning look my way.

I shrugged. "She was elderly and most likely had dementia."

"Why fix her car at all, then?" she asked.

"He helped her sell it," Xan provided the answer when I was slow to. "She still had payments to make on the thing, but clearly shouldn't be driving anymore. So, Miles fixed it, sold it, covered the costs of the parts and her payments, and then gave her the rest."

"There were only a few hundred bucks left. She needed it more than we did," I muttered, hating how much the guys needled me about being a softie when it came to the elderly.

"You're right, Alpha," Xan replied startling me with his sincerity. "It was the honorable thing to do."

I rolled my eyes. "No need to lay it on so thick, man." I clapped Xan on the shoulder. "Akela isn't meeting me for the first time. You don't have to talk me up. She's here to get to know all of you better."

"I'm not so sure about that," Luke spoke for the first time.

Akela looked his way, but not before I noticed her chewing on her lip as those bottomless blue eyes contemplated me.

"Perhaps Akela has never known you at all," Luke added.

"Why do you say that?" she challenged with raised chin.

It wasn't Luke that answered, though, surprisingly it was our omega that championed me hardest. "Because," Kyle spoke barely above a whisper. "If you knew him, there was no way you would have waited this long to be with him."

I held my breath, both deeply touched and annoyed his response might set her off and end a pleasant moment. Akela shifted forward in her chair resting her elbows on the table and leaning in. I could feel the alpha presence in her response to being challenged. Amazingly, Kyle held his ground. He didn't retract his statement, look away, or hunch over.

"What if I knew things you didn't?" Akela raised an eyebrow while addressing him directly.

A sad smile played on Kyle's lips. "You should try us. State the worst, but only if you are prepared to hear our truth as well."

My mate tilted her head to the side. A thoughtful expression danced over her delicate features. "Fine by me. I've always hated small talk. Might as well just jump into the deep end, seeing as the full moon is tomorrow night." She leaned back in her chair and met the gaze of each of the guys. "I'll tell you plainly my reservations about this pack or Miles, and you tell me why I'm wrong. That the game?"

"I'm not so sure," I jumped in. The last thing I wanted was a fight. We were so damn close.

She reached over and touched my shoulder. "No matter what is said, I promised I'd stay for the change. I stand by that promise. My wolf will run with your pack. I can't promise the pack bonds will form, though. Maybe this is what we need."

I could feel my heart beating inside my chest, the pulse thrum in my neck. I scrubbed my face with both my hands. "Ugh! Fine."

"Tate is closer to me than my own brothers and Miles abandoned him to die as a kid. That is a big one in our family." Akela's pinched lips signaled this was all she truly needed to know about me.

"Did Tate say that to you?" I had to ask. My brother was only four when I took him to Alpha Austin's property. I guess there was a chance he forgot what really happened that night.

"No," she conceded. "He says you were supposed to drag him far into the woods and get him good and lost, but you ended up near our property."

Able, the only one besides Dex that came from my former pack, spoke up. "You only have part of the story right. Social worker was poking into things and stopping by for visits. Full moon was coming and Tate was too young for the change. Their omega left them for another pack. His mom didn't want a human social worker finding a four-year-old boy all alone for days. Miles's mother told him to lose his brother in the woods and hope for the best. Miles was just seven years old at the time. What does he do? Listen to the scariest, meanest alpha ever known? Nope, he defies her. Packs up his brother, takes him by bus, and delivers him to the doorstep of your pack. As a seven-year-old! He knew you'd take Tate in and care for him. He gave up the only family member that gave a damn about him, so Tate could be safe. Then he spent the next five years getting the crap beat out of him because of it, by his mother, his father, and his brothers."

"What are you saying?" Akela's face pinched and her eyes bounced between mine and Abel's.

"I didn't realize everyone in the old pack knew," my voice was hoarse as if I'd been the one doing all the speaking.

"We saw it happen. She hated the Austin pack, and she made sure you suffered for taking Tate to them. She whined to my mother over how her own flesh and blood made her look weak. She was cruel to you. At least until you showed signs of being an alpha. Then her cruelty took on the guise of sculpting you to take over the pack someday." Able faced Akela directly. "I'll admit to being a bit of a fuck up. Growing up where Miles and I did, does things to you. I'm just a year younger than Tate, you know. I used to wish I had a brother like Miles who gave a crap about me. When I heard Dex joined up with him, I left that viper pit of a pack the first chance I could. Miles is an alpha that cares for his pack and puts their welfare first."

I could see this information was a great deal for Akela to take in. She kept rubbing at an imaginary spot on the table while she processed Abel's words. I'd told her in the past I never would have or could have hurt my brother, but this old prejudice was a hard one to erase. I reminded myself she was as much shaped by her pack's feelings as I was by mine.

"What about Dex? He always tells me you are going back there and taking over the pack. Are you going to promise me you won't? Will you give up any revenge fantasy or…?"

"Yes," I answered decisively.

"That quickly?" She appeared skeptical.

"What Dex says and what I plan to do are very different things. I have no revenge fantasy. I have no plans to kill my father. I want a different kind of pack. I want this pack." Glancing at the group around the table, I saw a bunch of loner guys that were once strangers, but now closer to me than my own family.

"I have heard you say the meanest things to him." She blinks owlishly before some heat returns to her glare.

I winced as she struck a nerve. I always felt like such shit about that. "It kept my mom away. Kept me from being the family's punching bag. Kept Tate safe from her thinking about taking him back. If I treated him like garbage, then it was the right thing to do when she threw him away."

Akela shook her head in denial. "So what?" she scoffed. "You were the perfect mate all along and I was the asshole?"

"I never claimed to be the perfect anything." I wanted to jump out of my skin. This conversation made me fidget in my seat. I don't like talking about my childhood, and I hated the doubt in her eyes. No one had ever believed I was capable of anything but brute strength and anger. Looking at my pack made me amend that—no one until this pack of misfits came into my life, that is.

"You sell yourself short, Miles. You're a decent guy and Austin's pack has been giving you a bad rap for years." Kyle bitterly spit out Austin's name. Our stoner omega was known for always being chill. His burst of anger surprised and flattered me. "They are blinded by old prejudice."

I could tell my mate's first reaction was to deny any wrongdoing the glorious Saint Austin or his perfect pack might have done, yet she refrained and started to study me intently. The crease between her brows alerted me she was trying to puzzle it all out.

I felt uncomfortable for her. The urge to put her at ease for seeing me always as a sack of shit. "I have a temper," I admitted solemnly.

"Every alpha has a temper," she muttered.

"I live paycheck to paycheck.." I gestured around our thrift-store-decorated cabin. It was a far cry from the rich pack life she was used to.

"Because he's the only mechanic in a fifty-mile radius with a conscience when it comes to charging customers," Able interjected.

"My pack consists of a compulsive thief, an omega stoner, a sex addict, a quiet loner, and worst of all, a California hippie."

"Hey!" Xan laughed.

"The *worst* would be Dex." Akela consolingly patted Xan on the shoulder. The action was playful but her words held her truth. I couldn't write off the things Dex had said and done. The guy was the first to join me, letting go of the comfort of pack bonds for a lone-wolf lifestyle. I felt a sense of loyalty to him for that sacrifice. It worried me she might never accept him. Maybe giving her a laundry list of all my weaknesses wasn't the smartest move.

"Hey." I held out my hand to my mate as I stood. "Let me show you around the property."

She reached for me without any show of hesitation. Her hand was warm and soft. "I'd like that." She smiled almost shyly as I dragged her away from any more heavy topics.

Chapter Fifteen

Six Months Ago

I had just finished sliding in new brake pads and retracting the pistons when my phone blew up. I could hear several texts pinging me in rapid succession. I knew they were all from Akela, hers was the only phone I allowed to alert me during business hours. Unfortunately, the guys knew it too.

"Oh, Lover Boy?" Caius called out. "Guess it's time to quit it so you can go hit it!"

Inwardly I groaned as the garage filled with kissing noises and sexual grunts. "Cut it out!" I growled. "A little respect, please."

"When you bring her around and introduce her to the pack," Xan began the broken-record speech that I might have hated more than the teasing. "We promise to be on our best behavior."

"Speak for yourself," Dex grumbled. "I have no interest in trying to impress that prissy pack princess. She should be crawling to us and begging for our pack's forgiveness for her shit treatment of our alpha."

"Oh, I think she treats him to something good," Caius cackled. "She got them banned from the Silver Crest Motel with one hell of a noise complaint and a broken bed."

I checked the brake fluid level and straightened up. It took little more than a dark silent stare down to finally get them to shut it. I washed the grease off my hands before I read the messages. I saw the name of yet another motel making me a bit forlorn. This routine of ours was getting old. My mate kept me out of every facet of her life except when she wanted a booty call. The guys were right. It was time she met them. I'd tried over the years to get her in a public place where they could casually join us, but Akela never agreed to be seen in public with me. I was all for patience at one time, but at this rate we would never be a true pack. That may not have been a burning desire in me a few years ago, but I was in a different place now. I bought the garage off of the old owner Doug five years back. The place made enough money to support us, we had a decent cabin in a very pretty area for the change, and heck, we even had an omega to make it feel like a home away from home. I was ready to step this up, but wasn't sure how to get my girl as invested.

"Where's the sexcapade being held this time?" Dex never could learn when to shut his trap.

"Lay off, I'm not in the mood," I warned.

"Uh-oh!" Caius covered his mouth feigning shock. "I hope that wasn't what you texted … I mean sexted her." Snorts and muffled laughter filled the garage.

I gave them the finger. "Feel free to finish the brake on the other side. Ms. Granger is coming at seven in the morning to pick up her car. I'll see you ass clowns on Monday." There was no griping about me cutting out at two on a Friday and leaving them with my work. Even if we were not a true pack yet, I was still alpha. The guys did not feel used or belittled for taking on anything I left them. Those were exclusively human emotions. In pack life, when an alpha asked, the pack complied. It was as ingrained as breathing. If only I could manipulate that into getting them to stop harping on me about Akela.

Problem with that request was simple. It was in the best interest of the pack if I brought her in. The guys would never cross the line and demand anything of me, but I tolerated the constant pestering. My relationship was fucked up. It was my job to fix it. It was my responsibility to make us a pack in all ways. Alphas put pack needs before their own.

I mulled it over a few times as I drove home and showered. I knew it was time to bring all of this up with Akela. I also knew it most likely would not end well. I grabbed a duffle bag and tossed in a change of clothes and a toothbrush. My eyes traveled to a white box sitting on the nightstand. At one time, it had a shiny purple bow. When I first brought it home over a year ago, I hadn't imagined it would take this long to give it to her. It was a bit dusty and stained on the edge where I spilled coffee one morning. Maybe this weekend wasn't the right time. I should at least rewrap it. I huffed out a loud gust of air and yanked it off the dresser. Tearing off the dirty bow, I opened the box and stuffed the contents in my pants pocket. It felt like a now-or-never moment. Or some other saying like it.

I texted I was on my way, slung my bag over my shoulder, and marched to my car wondering how the hell I was going to do this. Should I instantly set the tone and force a serious talk about our future? Tell her it wasn't fair stringing me along all these years. We were not human, we were true mates. There would be no one else for us ever. Why continue to torture ourselves?

With my speech firmly rehearsed on the ride over, I psyched myself up a few minutes more before I slid the plastic card into the motel room lock. *Stick to the plan. Don't get side tracked. State clearly your expectations. Tell her it is time. Don't accept no for an answer, again.*

That plan went right out the window when I stepped into the hotel room and saw Akela naked, touching herself. Cognitive thoughts evaporated with the erotic image. She was so damn sexy.

"Hope you don't mind. You were taking so long

to get here, I might have started without you." The little minx burned me with her bedroom eyes. My mouth went dry. I was instantly hard. She certainly captured my full attention with her show.

Swinging her long toned legs off the bed, Akela stood up and prowled over to me. I continued to stand still, mouth open, like a dolt. Her lips twisted to the side in a sly smile. She knew the power she wielded over me. Her hand grabbed at the waistband of my jeans, fingers brushing the tip of my cock as it strained against the denim. She yanked my underwear and pants down in a rough tug. Nails scratching against my thighs, humming in appreciation as she looked me over. I supposed we could have the life-altering serious talk later?

Decision made, I switched to the aggressor, pushing her back onto the mattress and burying my face between her thighs. The ragged moans and gasps she made spurred me on. Her hand buried in my hair, fingers glided over my scalp, causing goose bumps to run down my neck racing to the end of my spine. We might have set a record for how fast she came, lending credence to her story about her pre-game warm-up.

While the waves of her orgasm continued to roll over her, I sunk into her wet heat. "Damn," I muttered. "I missed you so fucking much."

Her sultry laugh was followed up with a nip to my earlobe. "It's only been two weeks."

A day apart from my mate was too long, but I knew better than to say that out loud. I lifted her hips angling them the way I liked and set a fast pace lasting only long enough to bring Akela to round two, before I found my release.

After the cloud of lust no longer fogged up my brain, I rolled next to her and quietly stared at the ceiling. I needed to think of the pack. Akela sat up and looked at me funny. She chewed on her lower lip for a bit while the silence remained.

"Okay," she raised an eyebrow while she spoke. "What gives? You just went from hot to cold like my gram's shower when the toilet flushes."

"What are we doing?" I huffed out the question.

"Well, we were having a good time," she drawled. "Now, I think you're having a sulk?"

"Is this all you want in life? Did you dream as a girl of a future of occasional hookups in dingy motel rooms?"

Akela grabbed a pillow and hugged it to her chest, effectively covering herself from me. "No," she softly admitted. "But I'm working with the cards I was dealt."

"What the hell is that supposed to mean?"

The constant confidence my mate wore crackled before my eyes. "This is where we're good." She gestured around the room. "But out there, too much gets in the way."

I sprung out of bed and fished my discarded pants from the floor, pulling a necklace from the back pocket. Then I proceeded to do the least romantic thing I could with it. I tossed it on the bed as if holding it burned me. Akela shimmied further up the bed as if fearful the ceremonial jewelry would touch any part of her.

"It's time, Akela."

She shook her head mulishly. "No."

Rage coursed through me. I welcomed it far more than I would despair. "And why the fuck not?"

"You mean, besides the way you asked me to be your mate?" she snarked.

"You. Are. My. Mate!" the words came out angry and clipped.

She reached for the mating necklace and threw it

at me. I caught it on reflex. It took a considerable amount of willpower not to throw it back.

"You know what I mean," she huffed. "Yes, we are mates," she bitterly snarled. "But wearing that means I accept your claim and I agree to leave my pack and join you."

"I know what it fucking means!" I walked back to the bed and sat beside her. I slowly counted down in my head until I could breathe without choking. Gently, I held the necklace out to her. "I got you this because I am asking you to accept me."

A single tear slid down her perfect porcelain skin. She couldn't meet my eyes when she rejected me. "I could never do that to Tate. He's family. I love him."

"Akela," I whispered her name as if it pained me. "Tate can't be an excuse you use. He's not even part of Austin's pack anymore. Tate is my brother. I know him. He will understand our need to be together. He will not think you chose me over him."

"You don't know that for sure," she said and sighed heavily. "My family might never speak to me again. You didn't care about leaving your family. You don't know what it is like for me to be worried about not seeing them again."

"Maybe not, but what I do know is you are an *alpha* female. There will be a day soon when Valentina will force you out. Even if you have hidden us away and she believes she is sending you out to be a lone wolf, it will happen. She will put the pack's welfare above yours. You already must be at each other throats."

"That's not good enough a reason to burn the bridges with my family and have them despise me." She went back to hugging the pillow for comfort. "As a lone wolf I can still go home, still visit during the holidays, and hang with Raf's pack too.."

"Being with me doesn't mean you can never see them again."

"Oh? And what of my parents? Alpha Austin? What if they decide being with you isn't all right?" She challenged me, yet I could see the stark fear widening her eyes.

"I know our family packs have been enemies, but we are true mates. They have to accept it," I pleaded with her. "They would not be so cruel as to prefer you be alone and isolated from all of our kind."

"Why risk it?" She dropped the pillow and reached for the hand I grasped the necklace with. My offering still being held to her. She slowly curled my fingers over the jewelry and pushed my arm down. "We have something right now. Why is this so terrible? I see you, we have fun, the mate bond settles. Let's not throw it away for something else that will hurt us both."

"Secret hookups in remote motels? This isn't pack life." I looked around the room in disgust. Disgusted that this was all she wanted to give me. Disgusted at myself for always hoping she would want more. I stood up and hopped into my jeans, shoving the necklace into my back pocket. "Am I mean to you? Cruel? Treat you in any way that makes you feel less than?"

Still kneeling on the bed, she silently shook her head.

"Then, tell me what we have is real. Tell me I'm worthy of you. Stop making me feel like a piece of trash. Maybe there was a time when we were kids that I could accept it, but not now. Not when you are all I fucking think about, even when you treat me like crap." I crossed my arms over my chest waiting for her proclamation. Knowing I was setting myself up for disappointment, but heading over the cliff anyway.

She dared to look stricken at my words. "Don't make this into something ugly. You know I can't choose."

"Then I will." I found my shirt and hoisted up the unpacked bag I left right by the door. "I'm done with this. No more booty calls."

"You are going to hold out on me?" she scoffed. "The urge to be together will make that resolution crumble."

I sighed. It was totally going to suck, but as my mate said earlier, I had to play the hand I was dealt. "I can't even imagine another guy saying this but here it goes. I'm too easy. I'm a sure thing. I answer every text and drop my entire world to be with you. When you want me next, you must work for it."

She pulled the pillow back to cover herself. "I can be a camel," she stated scornfully. "I am going to be able to hold out long after you crumble and crawl back to me."

I shrugged. "So you say." Closing the door between my mate and I was one of the hardest things I had ever done, but every good alpha puts pack first. I was determined to prove Akela wrong. I could stay away. I had to.

Chapter Sixteen

Present Day

The woods outside the cabin were fairly dense. The best part was you could walk for days in either direction and hardly ever run into a human. It was perfect for our three days under the full moon. I wanted Akela to feel acclimated with these surroundings. I knew from bringing in each new member of our pack it was a vital process to keeping their wolf safe when our human side wasn't in the driver's seat.

I pointed out various paths as we hiked and made sure to take her to all the locations we had woken up in when our wolves went dormant and we became men again. Those spots tended to be favorites of the pack's, close to water, game, and shelter. There was a river that flowed through the property, large enough to fish in, but small enough to still be able to cross on foot. Our wolves like this place best.

Akela gasped when we emerged from the trees. The light was sparkling off the water, prisms of rainbows floated in the air. The trees surrounding us dangled autumn leaves ranging from golden brown to fiery red. Large rocks created small spouts of white water as the river ran south. The current could pick up quite a bit after a heavy rain or at the end of spring when snow melt fed into it. During the summer months, the guys would come up a day or two early if possible and we would camp here and fish. It was the best thing our pack owned, and remote enough that no one else coveted it.

Akela's eyes sparkled with joy. Our inner wolves made nature lovers of us all. "It's so beautiful," she whispered in awe.

My heart constricted painfully. She was the most

exquisite thing in this world. "Nothing truly holds a candle to your beauty."

Surprise graced her features at my compliment, before her cheeks adorably reddened. Then the joy was snuffed out, replaced by a look of utter sadness. Icy tendrils dripped down my spine to see it. Was it regret? Did she miss her family? Not able to control the instinct, I reached for her and gently cupped her cheek in my hand. "What's wrong?"

She huffed out a laugh and wiped at her watery eyes. "I spent so much time trying to hate you. I was worried about being the good girl and falling for the bad boy. I blamed my wolf for making me want someone so terrible."

My hand fell away as her words pierced me. She didn't let me move far, though. She grabbed my hand, placing a kiss over my knuckle. "The reality was I made you into the poster boy for 'all good guys finish last.' I was such a bitch to you. Using you when I needed it. Never giving a crap about what that was doing to you, or our bond. Refusing to believe what was right in front of me the entire time."

"We are both products of our former packs," I stated wanting to console her.

She shook her head ruefully. "I am, but you aren't. The prejudice my pack holds for your old pack ran deeper than it should have. I wish I agreed to meet the guys sooner. Seeing you through their eyes was a revelation. I always wanted to be with you, even when I acted like I didn't. I thought it was a betrayal to Tate, even though he never said a thing to mc about it."

She took a shaky breath about to say more. A secret still dampened the light in her eyes. "It was a relief when you kidnapped Chloe," she continued. "It let me be a martyr. I played at being the self-sacrificing alpha, saving another. Truly, though, it gave me the excuse I needed to give into my cravings to be with you."

The talk of cravings had heat replacing all the ice that had formed around me. "All I want is you, Akela. I never gave up on that dream."

"No thanks to me." She smiled forlornly. "You have more patience than anyone gives you credit for. I'm ashamed that I never considered giving you a chance. For that, I am truly sorry. We may have a star-crossed lover's story, but what we have is real."

Those words were wondrous music to my ears. Circling my arms around her waist, I kissed her deeply. She was sweeter than the cinnamon and sugary breakfast she baked me. Her hands clasped around my neck as she pressed her body tighter into mine. Our mate bond was a live wire in my chest, sending jolts of pleasure back and forth between us. She sighed in-between kisses as her final barriers melted away. The mate bond was strong, flowing from her to me like a happy pulse. The absence of the pack bonds didn't worry me. It would take her shifting with us, before I would be able to feel them. Before my girl could make us all whole. She would turn this pack into a family. I firmly believed it.

I reached into my back pocket and pulled out the ceremonial mate necklace I'd gotten for her. Her eyes watered a bit seeing it in my hands. "I did this all wrong last time," I confessed.

"You said what you needed to." She dabbed at the tears cresting her cheeks. "I was cruel."

"If you agree to accept my claim and take my pack as your own, I promise to never hold out on you again. Sex on demand. Wherever. Whenever." I delivered the line perfectly deadpan and Akela went from crying to laughing in an instant. Her joy fueled my own. She lifted her long blonde hair up, signaling she wanted me to put the necklace on. I'm embarrassed to admit my hand shook slightly getting the clasp to close. Seeing my claim around her throat, though, gave me a primal sense of satisfaction.

"Let's put your pledge to the test. Looks to me like we still have an afternoon to kill before the moon rises. This woman has some demands to make." She wiggled her eyebrows comically while leering at me suggestively. She was clowning, of course, but I was a man of my word.

"Yes, ma'am!" I scooped her up and slung her over my shoulder fireman style and trotted back to the cabin with my mate giggling and swatting playfully for me to put her down.

Chapter Seventeen

Two Weeks Ago

"He fucking what?" I asked Caius to repeat himself.

We were crammed into my apartment by the shop. Caius had requested a pack meeting. "They finally got that serum to work. Raff kidnapped his true mate and injected her with it. She can shift now."

Luke nodded along, having heard the news as well. "Alpha Austin is overjoyed. He sent out a message for an all-pack meeting tomorrow welcoming her. She's the first sign of hope for those unable to shift."

"His son kidnaps a bitch and they celebrate. Austin's pack are such hypocrites," Dex scoffed.

For once, I one hundred percent agreed with Dex. It had been almost six months since I left Akela in a motel room because I wanted to have a true mate and not a side piece. She hadn't spoken a word to me since, a sure sign she thought I was beneath her and her perfect family. I knew her wolf was tearing her up inside being apart, because mine was going feral. "Seriously!" I bellowed, desperately wanting to punch something. "That is fucked up. Golden Boy can do no wrong, eh? Well, I gotta see this shit for myself."

"Sweet!" Dex looked positively gleeful at my rage. "What's the plan?"

"It's an all-packs welcome meeting. We are a pack, even if Austin is unaware of the fact. I say we crash it and make ourselves known." The words sounded growly and ominous as I spoke. Here I was playing the hold-out suitor, while Boy Wonder up and stole his mate. Damn it all!

Kyle, being an omega, was always twitchy when

my ire was up. He usually would make himself as unobtrusive as possible, or get super stoned to deal. So, it shocked the hell out of me, when it was him that challenged my plan. "You're pissed, Miles. Are you sure it's a good idea to go?"

"Alpha Austin might see it as an act of aggression if we show up. We aren't an official pack. Not without bonds in place," Luke offered the reasonable argument.

"Well, our pack's alpha female will be there. If his son can be forgiven for abduction, who the hell is he to challenge us about a proper invitation?" Caius countered with similar simmering aggression.

"Exactly!" Dex crowed. "It's a stupid barbeque, not a wedding."

"Akela wouldn't like it," Kyle spoke sheepishly.

"Stop kissing her ass already, Omega," Dex snapped. "She doesn't even know you."

I held up my hand to stop the chatter. I didn't want them fighting when we all clearly had a common enemy. "Don't get your hopes up on her becoming alpha female anytime soon, man. Clearly, she'd rather torture herself than be with me." The bitter words slipped past my tongue and the room quieted. I'd been a beast to live with these last few months. Well, more beastly that is. It was hard to think straight, my wolf was riding me to see my mate. I tried not to take it out on the guys, but any mention of Akela would set me off. My mate had rejected me and I'd been busy licking my wounds. "I guess Raff doesn't surprise me much. He's Akela's cousin after all. He abducts his mate to get everything he wants, meanwhile, his fair cousin has been keeping our pack bonds hostage because she doesn't know what the hell she wants. They are both selfish fuckers."

"Miles," Xan looked troubled over my comparison. "Don't go and do something you will regret later." While Dex and Caius looked as upset as I did, Kyle, Able, and Luke were siding with Xan. They thought I was going to go off half-cocked and mess things up even more.

Part of me imagined they might be right. Nothing I had done so far had worked to convince my reluctant mate. The anger slowly drained as despair trickled in. "If fate itself cannot sway the ice queen, then nothing I do or don't do will have much effect."

Dex wrapped me with his knuckles on my shoulder. "Might as well have some fun, then, right? Rough up a few pretty boys, steal a few six-packs, put a nice damper on the"—he mimicked air quotes—"happy occasion."

Normally I would shut down Dex's ideas. His brand of fun hit too close to home, reminded me too much of our old pack life. Today, it fit my mood. I wanted to create havoc. If I wasn't ever getting my happily ever after, why should Raff, an entitled prick, get his? "I could use some fun." I grinned picturing crashing the party in a spectacular manor.

"Wow, slow down, Alpha," Able, our resident thief, called for caution. "Showing up for some free food and drink is one thing. I'm all for robbing from the rich alpha to feed our sorry asses, which goes without saying, but Luke's right. We aren't an official pack. Entering Austin's territory will be seen as an act of aggression. He might think you're there to try and overthrow him or steal his stupid formula."

"So what?" Dex puffed up his chest. "First off, besides Snow White here," Dex singled out Luke, the only arctic wolf in our gang. "Most of us are Greys. Bigger, faster, stronger, baby. They are Reds, clever for sure, but no match for us head-on."

"So, we are going to war now?" Xan questioned

solemnly.

Our omega, who only enjoys two things—writing code or getting stoned—freaked out at the idea of violence. "We can't do that!"

"Sitting around and waiting for Princess Charming isn't getting us any closer to being a pack," Caius taunted him.

While I was spoiling for a fight and burning up about the unfairness of it all, the bottom line was I still wanted my mate. Scrubbing my hands over my face I growled out my frustration. "I need to at least confront her."

Xan put a calming hand on my shoulder. "She has wronged you, brother. She doesn't see the alpha you are. Whether she accepts you or not, you have made us a pack. Even if we never feel whole, if we are meant to be together but incomplete, it's still enough."

Luke put his pale hand next to Xan's brown one. "You are our alpha, and we are your pack."

Even Caius's rigid shoulders dropped. "Whatever happens, Miles, we got your back."

"I need to see her. I need to see if this changes anything, but I won't go in guns blazing." I tried to portray the confidence they expected from an alpha.

"Well." Dex folded his arms over his chest. "You aren't going in alone. I'm coming as backup."

He probably wasn't the best choice. Luke or Xan would be cooler under pressure. Dex was the first to join me in packless life and I felt I owed him this opportunity to be my wingman. "All right, then. Just me and Dex are going. Caius, find out what time this gathering is. I say a fashionably late entrance will set the right tone."

****

The garage was usually a thirty-minute drive to Austin's lands but I was so riled up I did it in twenty. I

133

didn't stop flooring it until I was on the pack's cul-de-sac, barreling past the row of neat white houses, I saw the grand old farmhouse at the end. I'd never been invited inside. The closest I ever got was when I dropped four-year-old Tate off at the end of the street in the middle of the night. This night, I didn't cower or hide. I refused to slow down when I entered the driveway, launching my monster truck over the curb and demolishing the pristine manicured rosebushes. It's all just a facade to cover up the rot inside. This entire pack was insufferably superior, yet they were no better than criminals. First it was turning Tate against me, then making my mate feel like she could never accept me, and now celebrating the golden boy's mate abduction with a flashy party. I was sick of carrying the weight of my former pack on my shoulders. The sins of my parents were not my own. If they were going to hate me, well, then let it be for my own actions.

"Hilarious!" Dex was cutting up beside me in the truck bed. Hooting at the destruction I was causing, he appeared to be having the time of his life. In fact, I couldn't recall a time he was happier.

A raven-haired beauty swung open the door to shoot a pointed look at the rosebushes we crushed. I didn't recognize her from any past events. It certainly wasn't Valentina, the pack's female alpha. I threw open the car door and stood at my full height. I knew how imposing I looked. Giant, overly muscled, tatted up and covered in oil from the shop, my presence alone would be intimidating, but add the roided-out look that Dex sported alongside me, it was no surprise when her features morphed from fury to fear.

She showed no sign of recognizing me, and it dawned then who she was. "You must be Raff's."

Leaning against the doorframe, she folded her

arms under a very sizable rack. "I am," she replied more calmly than her breathing indicated she was feeling. "Can I help you?"

"I greatly doubt it," I scoffed. I wasn't here to gawk at the medical breakthrough. I wanted Akela to come out and face me.

"Ah, come on now, Miles." Dex sidled up beside me "She looks like she could be at least good for something." The look of disgust she threw his way was a mistake. Dex liked nothing better than antagonizing women who thought they were too good for him. When she took a step away, I heard him hum in satisfaction at the sight. I had to settle him before he got too out of hand.

"Cool it, Dex." I patted his shoulder. "I hardly think this science experiment is worth the trouble."

The front door banged open and my mate stormed out to the porch. Even though her deep-blue eyes were spitting fire, something in my chest calmed at seeing her. Over five months was simply too long to be away. My Viking goddess, hand thrust on hip, wild golden wavy hair tossed over her shoulder, was not pleased to see me, though.

"What the hell are you assholes doing here?" she hissed. "Leave before Tate or Austin catches sight of you."

That's what she had to say to me? After almost six months! There was no way in hell I was leaving before we talked. "You planning to make me, little girl?"

She rolled her eyes looking disgusted. "You're not welcome here."

"That's funny." I acted confused. "I heard all packs were welcome to behold the manufactured miracle." That comment got the raven-haired doll's spine to stiffen and Akela looking even more annoyed at my presence. I should have added that she knew damn well we were pack and that's why I was there.

Akela put her hands on her hips and did that perfect "fuck off and die" head tilt that only a woman can execute flawlessly. "Leave before someone sees you."

That's right, because I'm the embarrassment here, her true mate she rejected so casually, leaving my soul in tatters. My entire body felt like an erupting volcano. It was past time they all saw me for what I was. An alpha of a pack needed his mate. "Maybe I want to be seen."

Akela huffed and her eyes darted toward the backyard. "Careful what you wish for, Miles. You two ass-clowns might be the size of woolly mammoths, but there are still only two of you."

As if her words signaled them, Raff, his pack, and all his younger brothers spilled onto the porch. Raff took a protective stance in front of his mate. "What are you doing here, Miles?"

I didn't give two shits about the alpha speaking to me. My mate wanted me gone, but what about my brother? Tate stood shoulder to shoulder with Akela. He was the only one on the porch not throwing daggers with his eyes at me. I acknowledged him with a nod. "Started my own pack, Tate. If you're done playing house with these rejects, you should come join me. We have seven pack members now." My eyes floated over Akela. "Soon to be eight, better than Raff's little pack of five."

"You mean six," Raff's mate scowled.

Considering she only recently became one, I doubt she really counted. "You aren't a real shifter."

"Not this crap!" Akela hissed. "You are just like your family! Always looking for a weakness to stamp out. Throwing away Tate like he was garbage!" Akela's face mottled red. She dropped her arms and clenched her hands into fists.

I tried not to grind my teeth down to stubs. It didn't matter what I did or said to this woman, it always came down to Tate. The stench of my parents' actions would never leave me. Akela wanted to believe the worst in me. She never bothered to judge me on my actions as an adult, but the crap I had no control over when I was just a kid.

"I don't understand you at all, Miles." Tate was solemn. "If this piece of shit represents your pack,"—he pointed at Dex—"it doesn't speak very well of you, brother."

His words were a direct hit. The one person I loved as a kid was Tate, yet just like Akela, he never picked me. Dex might be an absolute asshole, but he picked me. I glared at Tate, not wanting him to see how much his disdain hurt.

"Look at that!" crowed Dex. "Lil Tate thinks he finally grew himself some balls. You a real man now, boy?"

Tate ignored the comment and returned my cold stare. "I believe my alpha asked you what you were doing here."

I wanted to say I didn't feel disappointed at him calling Raff his alpha, but I'd be lying. I had always hoped one day he would join me and we could be a family. Instead, yet again, it would be the golden boy who got it all. Dismissing my brother with a shake of my head, I leered at Raff. "Since your pack has decided to create its own women, I came to see if any of the true she-wolves left would finally stop pitying you all and leave with some real shifters?" A barely audible breath escaped Akela, but I could see I struck a nerve.

The tick in Raff's jaw was working overtime. "Sticks and stones, man. It's sad how your family won't evolve from the bullies on the playground. Our kind is dying out and you treat it like it's a race to the finish."

Fuck this. I wasn't getting anywhere. No matter what I had to say, they had already judged me.

"Well, Dex," I drawled. "I guess we're not invited to the barbeque."

Dex grabbed at his heart and winced. "That hurts," he mocked.

Raff was about to speak again, but I cut him off. "Don't bother." I gave Akela one last hard stare. She stood facing me coolly, lips pressed in a firm thin line. She would not relent. "I saw all I needed to." I turned back to my truck, nodding at Dex to follow. Coming here was stupid.

"He doesn't bother me, babe," I heard Raff's mate croon

"Of course not, darlin'. He's less than dirt compared to you," Raff's response was almost enough for me want to go back and pound on his ass, but I had a better idea forming. One that would make him shit his pants in fear and finally know what it felt like to lose.

Dex turned and gave a cocky wave before he slid into the truck with me. "I say good riddance, man. The guys are all in agreement, we don't need her to be a pack. Fuck her."

I threw the truck in "reverse," demolishing more roses on my way back down the drive. "I'm not calling it quits, Dex."

"Ah, man…" Dex bashed his head against the seat. "At some point it's just plain pathetic."

"Don't worry," I grunted shifting gears. "I'm not planning on asking next time. If it worked for Golden Boy, then I say why not try?"

Chapter Eighteen

Present Day

My toes were half frozen, but my chest felt like it was cuddled up with a soft warm blanket. The smell of coconut and the trickle of running water nearby forced my brain to focus. I was in the woods. Waking up after a shift was a hazy adventure at best. Fragments of memories peppered my conscious thoughts. Dex had not returned in time for the shift. Akela had kept her promise. She had greeted the moon with the pack. The guys had been giddy with joy howling with their human voices at the moon while we all stripped and waited for the change. The actual change was never a clear memory, but after there had been a scuffle or maybe a hunt gone wrong during our time as wolves. As the alpha, I could sense I had acted in the pact's defense, but that was all I could piece back together.

The warmth blanketing me was my mate, naked like me, and curled into a ball, head resting on my sternum. The scent of her shampoo still strong even after being outside for the past three days inhabiting another body. My arms circled her. My fingers threaded through her hair, dislodging twigs and dead leaves. "Morning, sweetheart."

"Ah, shucks, Alpha." Caius sat up on the other side of me scrubbing his face. "Morning right back at ya!"

Akela snorted at his antics and stretched out like a cat before sitting up. She angled her slender neck in small circles, working out the kinks caused by nights on the uneven ground. Kyle and Luke were huddled close to her other side. Not something the human in me enjoyed seeing, but I made allowances for our wolves. They slept in one big pile for warmth and it kept us from waking up frozen to death. Even though the guys were little better than strangers, Akela took the closeness in stride. She was comfortable in her own skin.

My eyes scanned the pack for any injuries. It wasn't uncommon to wake up with a cut or bite mark from our three-day adventure. Everyone was muddy and a bit befuddled, but otherwise unharmed. Dex was nowhere in sight. This was unusual. I thought his wolf would find us after the shift, even though he was apparently still too pissed off to join us before it took place. We did not possess true pack bonds, but his wolf always stayed with the pack.

"Anyone remember seeing Dex?" My mouth tasted foul and I scrubbed at my teeth with the back of my hand. There was coarse fur in my mouth. Most likely from an animal I killed for the pack to eat. One of the more unpleasant side effects of our lifestyle. As alpha, I usually woke up the bloodiest. Alphas provided.

Xan was the first to stand and scout out the situation. His thick black hair and the entire left side of his face was caked in mud. He managed a quick braid and swatted at the mud on his cheek while talking. "We aren't too far from the cabin. Maybe a half-mile. Perhaps he woke up elsewhere and headed back?"

"I'm desperate to jump in the river and get off this mud," Akela grimaced as she looked at her hands. "Do you have a clothing stash nearby?"

I sat up and nestled my forehead against hers. The mate bond thrummed happily when she didn't pull away, leaning into me instead.

Kyle bounced up. "I'll get you something!" He raced off to the bear locker we kept about a hundred yards away. "There should be some trail mix in there too as well as clothes."

Akela beamed at our omega, as he eagerly scurried off to care for his pack. "Thanks, Kyle, you're the best." She sang-spoke to him causing a heady high look to overtake his expression. Considering the kid was such a stoner, it was an expression I often saw him wear, just never while totally sober. As I looked at the pack, he wasn't the only one. All the guys had slightly glassy-eyed dopey dazed looks. Did our wolves eat some random mushrooms?

Luke clutched at his chest and sighed contentedly. "Thank you, Alpha."

I was confused about the appreciation, but realized he was speaking to Akela. She shook her head and laid a hand gently on his shoulder. "Never thank me for that. We are pack."

It all clicked then. I wasn't just feeling the heady happy vibrations of the mate bond, I was feeling the pack bonds forming around us. They were not ironclad yet, that came with time, but they strummed between us. It wasn't just Akela and me anymore, I could feel all the guys tethered to my soul. Luke's sense of relief at finally finding a permanent home, Caius's pride of our accomplishment, Xan's steady calm that everything would be better now, Able's glee of belonging, and Kyle's joy as he brought back the duffels from the locker knowing he would be making Akela as happy as he was now. Only Dex was missing.

"There are two towels in here, Akela. In case you want to jump in and get the dirt off before we hike it back. I also have a hoodie and sweatpants that will fit you." Kyle's eyes were bright as he pulled the offerings from the bag. Akela ruffled his hair before she wrapped the towel around her torso.

"Thanks again," She winked at me and a trickle of affection flowed down to the entire pack. "I'll just be, like, five minutes." She headed toward the trees in search of privacy. While our kind did not feel embarrassed at nudity, since it was a state we found ourselves in monthly, I assumed Akela, as the only female in our pack, required some alone time.

Kyle divvied out the contents of the duffels. I downed a bottle of water and tore into a granola bar, more eager to get the sour tang of blood out of my mouth than to get dressed. "I think I'll wait for hot water. Anyone else want to wash off before we head out?" I shoved my muddy legs into a pair of faded green sweatpants, cinching the waist slightly with a sloppy bow tie.

"Dang!" Caius whooped up at the sky. "We are a real pack." In a rare show of emotion, Caius patted his fist over his heart. "I didn't realize how much I missed feeling complete until I had it back," he spoke wistfully, his eyes misting. "Ah, man, its like I can draw a full breath again."

Luke offered him a gruff side hug. "I know. I've wandered a long time. This is the first place that feels like home. I'm lucky to call you my brothers."

A hoarse scream interrupted the touching moment. As one we sprinted in the direction Akela had gone. As alpha, I was naturally faster, so I outpaced the pack and arrived at the river a hundred yards ahead of the rest. The first thing I saw was Dex. He wasn't in good shape. Blood trickled down his face, it looked like his right ear was torn off. His chest was a series of slash marks. Jagged deep cuts that had to have been made by a rather large predatory animal.

He was standing in the middle of the river looking absolutely crazed, spittle flying from his lips as he yelled the same thing over and over. "Look what you did to me! This is your fault! You bitch! This is all because of you! Look what you did! Your fault."

Wildly I searched for Akela. The water around Dex was in upheaval, splashes caused by a flailing body. Dex had my mate by her neck and she thrashed while being held under. I saw red. In three leaps, I was able to tackle him and shove him away from Akela. When she came up gulping in a huge lungful of air, I frantically catalogued any other injuries she might have taken. She was shaken and gripping her throat as if it pained her, but otherwise intact.

There was shouting from the riverbank as our pack caught up with me. "Is she okay? Is that Dex? What the hell happened? Did Dex attack her?" I ignored it all. My beautiful mate had finally made us a pack, and less than an hour later we almost lost her. She could have died. My head swung in the direction of Dex. He was struggling to stand. The blood loss from his injuries, coupled with how hard I knocked him over, slowed down the giant of a man. I was on him before my brain could even process the movement. My fist connecting with his chin, punching him in the bloody mangled mess where his ear used to be. A scream erupted from him, but I did not stop pummeling. I always made allowances for Dex. Let everything he did and said slide because he was the first to join me in packless exile. Always feeling a sense of obligation for him, instead of what I should have. Disgust. He never hid who he was. I hadn't done much when he hurt Tate and his friend. There was no way in hell I would stand by while he tried to kill my mate. He didn't deserve to breathe.

"Miles," I could hear Akela's strained voice over Dex's moans. "I'm all right. Miles, you can stop. I'm fine. Miles, stop."

My hands circled around Dex's throat. While I squeezed, his arms shot up, hands too weak to pry me away. His eyes bulged. Terror etched across his features. Still, I squeezed. The pack watched silently on the riverbank. No one but Akela made a move to stop me.

Akela's hand rested on my shoulder almost gently. "Miles. You need to stop now. You're killing him. You're too good of a man for that kind of a stain. He's a piece of shit, but I know this will haunt you. Stop. Please."

Like a hypnotist snapping his fingers to wake another from a trance, the reality of my situation came rushing back to me. I sucked in air, released Dex's neck, and scrambled off of him. He coughed and spluttered out a mixture of blood and water, but he was still breathing. When I stood up fully, Akela circled her arms around my waist and laid her head on my chest.

"Oh, God…" I kissed the top of her head. "Are you okay? Where are you hurt?"

She murmured reassuring words to me, rubbing circles on my back trying to soothe me. The guys waded in and fished Dex out of the river. He collapsed as soon as he reached dry ground. I noted the dark stares and firmly pressed lips. If I had not attacked Dex one of them might have instead. There was no concern about his suffering.

I looked down at my mate. Guilt clawed at me. Here she was trying to calm me, when I should have been taking care of her. Her lips were blue, she was naked and shivering. I plucked her out of the water and carried her bridal-style to the others. Xan yanked off the hoodie he had on and pulled it over her head when I set her down. Kyle picked up the discarded towel at the water's edge and rubbed it quickly over her legs using the friction to warm her. Our pack bond doubled my worry with theirs for her condition.

"What happened?" I croaked out overcome with

so many emotions.

"I was washing up in the river. I didn't see Dex until he attacked me. He thinks my wolf kept him away from the pack when we shifted. That I challenged him for the pack territory and mauled him." She was hugging herself tight and chewing nervously on her lip. A tear slid down her cheek. "I can feel all of you in the bond, but I don't accept him as pack. I'm sorry, Miles. I know he's your lifelong friend, around even when I wasn't. I don't think I could ever bring him into the pack. I have an overwhelming instinct to push him away. He might be right. I might have hurt him."

"Of course it was you!" Dex scowled, but wisely continued to huddle on the ground showing no signs of aggression. "Look at me. My ear is torn clean off. I have claw marks all over me."

The muddled memories all clicked then. "It wasn't Akela."

"Of course it was," he moaned clearly in deep pain.

I shook my head. "It was me. My wolf cast you out. I remember glimpses of a struggle and I woke with fur and blood in my mouth." My stomach turned at the thought I might have eaten his ear. On closer inspection, my nails were caked with much more than mud. There was a definite copper tinge up to my knuckles.

"Then it was because of that bitch!" he hissed.

Angry mutterings rumbled through the pack at hearing Dex slander Akela. Strong feelings of gratitude and acceptance poured down the bond from the guys toward her. The pack had chosen. My girl straightened her spine and dried her eyes.

"What we do as our wolf selves cannot always be the fault of our human selves. We all know this. The way of the Wa'ya is to accept both halves of our natures," I stated calmly before my voice firmed. "What you did in attacking Akela, trying to drown her … you did that fully human. Fully aware."

"How can you take her side? Let her reject me as pack?" Dex sneered. "She has never wanted you. I left everything, my home and family to join you."

"Please," I scoffed. "You hated pack life and have never been fond of your family. I was convenient. I don't owe you anything. It was you that never accepted my mate. It's no surprise she rejects you. You hurt Tate and tried to kill her. She saved your life back there. I was the one that wanted you dead. She stopped me. Remember that, you miserable piece of shit! You owe her your life!" I scooped up my mate, loving the feeling of her in my arms too much to even consider letting her walk. "Don't come back to the cabin. You're no longer welcome on pack lands. And if you value your life, make sure you are at least a hundred miles from here the next change. My wolf is likely to finish what he started."

I turned and walked away, officially shunning Dex from our pack. I didn't care if the guys stayed to help him or give him a ride home, but I was done. After taking only a few steps, though, I heard them behind us and Dex screaming profanities about leaving him too weak to walk.

"If you were fucking strong enough to hurt our alpha female, then you're strong enough to take care of yourself!" Caius flipped Dex the bird and the others nodded in agreement. The pack bond was circling us, shoring up the exhaustion and fear we felt hearing Akela's panicked screams. Like a comforting group hug to help move us forward. We headed as one back toward the cabin.

Akela was silent for the first quarter-mile after I hushed her for stating she was fine and I should put her down to walk. Her legs were still shaking and the bruises forming on her neck made me unable to release her. At the halfway mark of our journey, she heaved a heavy sigh. Cradling her hand over my cheek, she stared at me. "Are you sure you are okay?"

I huffed at her question. "I should be asking you that. How's the throat? You have a necklace of bruises forming."

"Do we need to stop, Alpha?" Luke asked, concern etched over his face after seeing the evidence of my words.

"As much as I love the woods, if you don't get me back to some hot food and a comfy bed, I might really start to cry," Akela teased.

"If you are able to eat with your throat sore, I have a bag of almonds." Able shuffled forward and thrust them at her.

"You little thief!" Caius grumbled. "I pulled them out of the supply bag. I wondered where they vanished to."

Able shrugged sheepishly. "I didn't take them for me. You guys were scarfing everything down, so I just set them aside in case Akela came back looking for anything."

"Ahh…" She pinched Able's blushing cheek and happily took his offering. "What a gentleman." Both Caius and Xan snorted at that assessment. "Even though," Akela continued with a mischievous grin. "I've seen those sticky fingers in action at the liquor store, and I'm not entirely buying your altruistic story. But,"—she tossed a nut in the air and caught it—"I'm not one to look a gifthorse in the mouth." Able laughed alongside the others, not looking guilty in the slightest for getting called out. I marveled at how at ease she was with the pack. It had felt like an eternity to get her to meet them all and then a few short days later she tied us together and made us a family. We were no longer just headed to the cabin, now we were headed home.

****

I turned the shower to scalding before pulling Akela in with me. She had stopped shivering during the walk back, but the compulsion to care for her was riding me hard. I couldn't touch her, though, until I washed the blood from my hands and torso. She quietly contemplated my vigorous scrubbing for a minute before batting my hands away and taking over the duty herself. She was far gentler than me. Her mere presence was soothing. She hummed a Tammy Wynette song that had my mind finally disengaging from shunning Dex.

My lips tipped up as I watched her. "Stand by your man, eh?"

A delicate blush bloomed in her cheeks as her eyes searched mine. "Yeah, that feels about right. Something I should have done years ago but can only make it up to you now."

My heart kicked up its tempo. I was used to seeing her looking at me with lust and it was a great feeling, but seeing her look at me with respect might have been the headiest experience of my life. I leaned down to kiss her as she lifted on her toes to meet me halfway. She made a pleased little noise as my hands trailed down her body. I was instantly hard. I suck on her bottom lip, my teeth lightly nipping. Her hand settles around my cock, pumping till it weeps. I groan into her mouth. "I'm not able to get enough of you." She broke away from our kiss, and I almost protested the loss of her lips against mine, until she started sucking and licking up the side of my neck. A happy rumble to vibrate through my throat. Her hand threaded around the back of my head and she pulled me closer, her teeth nibbling my earlobe. This woman drove me wild. I wanted to pick her up and thrust inside her in one go, but the shower was too small to accommodate that fantasy.

Instead, she gave me another wet dream. Dropping to her knees, her hot mouth circled the head of my penis, her tongue pressed flat along the sensitive underside. I gripped the shower walls with both hands when she hollowed out her cheeks and sucked me in. My knees almost buckled from the sheer pleasure. "Fuck! I'm not going to last with you doing that."

I could feel her chuckle vibrate all around me, her happy hum letting me know she was thrilled to have me walking the precipice. Pleasure zinged down my spine and with iron willpower I had not realized I possessed, I pulled away from her amazing mouth. My cock sprang back against my abdomen just a few seconds away from exploding. I sleuthed the soapy water off us and turned the shower nozzle. "Bed. Now."

Her throaty chuckle had the fine hairs on my neck standing up. "Grab me a towel?"

"No time for that." I hoisted her up and she wrapped her legs around my torso. I loved hearing her laugh, but I was obsessed with hearing her moan. If she'd let me, I'd kidnap her for real, chain her to my bed, and spend weeks worshipping her body. The idea was so appealing, I just might.

I dropped her wet naked body on the bed and a fraction of a second later I had her spread before me. My mouth covered her clit and I sucked, hard. Her back bowed off the bed. "Oh my God!" she cried.

"Your turn," I grunted. My tongue rolled over that sensitive bundle of nerves, and a deep satisfaction resonated through me hearing her suck in ragged breaths. After adding a few fingers to the mix, she was a shaking panting mess. Her hands tugged at my shoulders prying me away. I looked up at her flushed smiling face.

"I need to feel you inside me," she purred.

I licked my lips still tasting her. "Needy little thing," I joked.

"Ha!" She winked backed. "Don't pretend you don't need me just as much." She rubbed at her chest. "I can feel it."

"Baby, there isn't a minute during the day that I don't want to be inside of you." To illustrate my words, I thrust inside her. She was soaking from my ministrations and welcomed me easily. Her soft wet heat gripped me. She threw her head back at the feel of me, exposing her long neck. Whether it was the beast I share this body with or myself, I couldn't resist biting her and feeling her pulse throb under my tongue. I kept her pinned as I pumped. She angled her hips higher so I could slide in deeper. Akela made these little mewling gasps alerting me that I reached just the right spot. I quickened my pace making sure to hit that perfect spot over and over until she screamed my name. Her legs were still shaking when I came. Her arms reached around me, nails scoring into my back to keep my chest flush with hers.

"Don't move," she whispered. "I need you to stay right there."

I gripped the side of her hip trying to bury myself as deep as I could. I feathered kisses from her brow, to the tip of her nose, onto both cheeks, until I reached her lips. My words were a breathy promise from my mouth to hers. "I love you. I'm not going anywhere."

****

Usually, the boys and I after a change spent the morning eating junk food and lounging around, but would leave the cabin before dark and head back to our normal lives. None of us seemed in any hurry this time. I hadn't scheduled any maintenance at the shop for two more days just in case we needed more time with Akela, convincing her to stay with us. Yet when the pack bonds started to form it was such a euphoric feeling, there was this need just to bask in it, relax for once. We hung at the cabin and our lazy Sunday turned into Monday and then Tuesday. We didn't want to leave and decided without speaking we would wait till the last minute before heading back. The pack living situation was more spread out than most packs would normally be. My apartment's proximity to Austin's pack went against their instincts. We would have to think of more permanent solutions. The need to be together, to be close, will be even greater with the bonds growing around us.

Luke had a shark documentary playing on the TV while we honest-to-God played a group game of *UNO* from an old deck Able had swiped from a pharmacy years ago. Kyle was in the kitchen cleaning up from lunch and making brownies, hopefully without the pot this time, since we would have to drive back tonight. Akela sat between my legs trying to keep her cards from my line of sight. I was busier looking down her top than giving a shit about her cards. Normally I would be way more competitive, can't stop the alpha inside me, but her perfect tits were a major distraction.

A loud banging on the front door halted our scene of domestic bliss. No one ever just showed up here. We were literally in the middle of nowhere. My first thought was that Dex decided to try to get back in our good graces, fat chance at that. Unfortunately, it was way worse.

"Miles," the perfect golden boy alpha bellowed outside my door. "I know you are in there. We are here for Akela."

My entire body went rigid as the entire pack looked at our female alpha for her response.

"Akela?" my brother called out next. "Can you come to the door?"

With a heavy sigh and a worried frown, Akela extricated herself from my lap and stood. The pack bonds grew taught as my pack stood as one and approached the door with her. A cold settled in my veins that I had hoped to never feel again. Akela always chose Tate over me. Why would this time be any different? The awful realization that my pack would also feel the devastation alongside me made this even worse.

I felt like "dead man walking" watching her swing open the front doors. The raven-haired beauty was surprisingly the first one through. "Akela!" she sobbed her name as she grabbed her in a tight hug and pulled her outside. The men of Raff's pack formed a tight ring behind them when my pack pushed through the door to surround them. We were close in number to Raff's pack, but while most of them were Reds, most of us were Greys. That meant we were bigger and meaner. I could see the determination of my pack to win this fight, but I understood there would be no victory that way. Akela either chose us or she chose them. She would break the bonds and walk away or declare that we were hers. I hadn't wanted a showdown to come so soon after our first shift together, but like a bandage, better to rip it off right away rather than wait for it to slowly pull free.

"Are you all right?" Raff's voice was gruff as he surveyed his cousin.

Akela was shaking her head side to side but she looked bewildered. "What are ya'll doing here?"

Tate looked a bit sheepish when he replied for their pack. "We came to rescue you."

"Huh!" Akela took a step back, her lips puckered in a small frown. "I don't need rescuing."

"You're happy in a pack with a man like Dex?"

Tate's voiced wobbled.

"Miles banished him. They all chose me with no reservation. Pack bonds don't lie. And I choose them."

The declaration created a collective sigh through our pack, as if we'd all been holding our breaths. Akela noted the sound and turned to face us. "I'm with my pack, exactly where I should be," she projected the words over her shoulder but they were directed at the guys and me. The bond in my chest singed me, she sent so much warmth flooding through it.

"Akela?" Chloe rested a hand on her shoulder. "Are you sure?"

"Are you?" Akela challenged back. Raff's mate's eyes widened at her tone. Akela's featured softened. "Look, sometimes alphas do stupid things all for the best of reasons. I'm sure you can appreciate that?"

Raff and his mate shared a look of understanding before Akela continued. Her eyes searched Tate's before she spoke. "I feel like we've unfairly judged your brother based on others' actions. He isn't your mother or father. He isn't your older brothers. This pack isn't like his old pack. When you first came to live with us, Tate, you idolized Miles. Told us all the time how wonderful he was. It was Austin and my folks that slowly made you feel like he betrayed you by leaving. They were worried about you going back to a place of abuse and believed he hurt you too."

"My older brothers were my biggest bullies. Miles never laid a finger on me," Tate agreed quietly.

Akela nodded. "These are some great guys with big hearts, and their alpha kept them together, kept them whole, even when the world told him he was trash. For years I was the one who used him and rejected him. I have known he was my mate since I was fifteen, but I never admitted it because of the prejudice against your biological family. I was the one who was terrible to him, it was never the other way around." Her admission was directed at Raff and Chloe. Her voice was clipped and firm. "He took it all in stride and accepted me, faults and all. Miles is my fated mate." She reached for me and threaded our hands together. "Only together are we truly complete." A solid lump formed in my throat. My beautiful goddess stunned me speechless.

Tate looked at me solemnly. "I don't remember much the night Jason died," his voice wobbled. "But I remember you were there."

I started to defend myself, but Akela held up her hand. "When I drove up he had your eldest brother pinned and Luke was trying to help Jason." She hung her head. "Another thing I royally fucked up. I blamed him that night too. But he had come out to stop them and rescue you. I should have told you when I found out, but you had left to join Raff's pack then and when I saw you next you looked better. You were overcoming your grief and I chickened out. Talking about that night was just too hard. I'm more at fault than Miles for Jason's death. I made you leave him there." She choked out the words, arms wrapped around herself tightly.

Tate reached for my mate and pulled her in a hug. "I never blamed you. You know that."

Tears streaked down Akela's face. "That is because you are an incredibly kind, caring, and forgiving person." Her head swung in my direction. "Just like your brother."

"I'm sorry for what you suffered, Tate. I should have kicked Dex out that night. He swore he had nothing to do with it. I should have known better. I never wanted you to get hurt. It's why I brought you to Austin's pack in the first place. You always deserved better than us." The old shame of feeling like an emotional dumpster made my voice wobble through my last sentence.

"Damn, Miles. Why the hell did we wait this long to just talk?" Tate sniffed and blew out a breath. "Are you happy with him, Akela?"

"I almost forgot what it felt like to be happy," she huffed. "I have been torn in two for so long. Worried about what my family would think instead of caring how much being away from my mate was hurting us both. Miles is my heart and my home. I think happy is only possible when I'm with him." She rubbed her chest. "I accepted these men as my pack. These bonds are ones I created because I believe this is my family now."

The swell of comfort, pride, and joy skittered along the bonds. I could sense Luke's contentment, Xan's relief, Able's happiness, Caius's pride, and Kyle's desire to care for us. A silly grin spread across Tate's face. He reached over and pulled me into their hug. "That makes me so happy. I trust you Akela. When you rejected Miles I assumed you had solid reasons. You're the sister of my heart, but I love you even more for bringing my brother back to me." Tate slugged at my arm. "I could never reconcile the brother of my memoires with the man our mother was so proud of. I thought she changed you," Tate's mouth pulled down and guilt swam in his eyes. "I judged you too. But I get it now. You did what you did to survive her, and you got away as soon as you could. I remember what you said when you left me with Austin's pack. That day has always stayed with me. You told me that truth isn't always something you can see clearly. That people do things they don't always want to do, but that doesn't mean they don't care. I'm sorry I let others blind me to your truth."

I rubbed the back of my neck with my free hand, feeling suddenly awkward in my own skin. "It's fine, man. Water under the bridge. I know I haven't made it easy for you to see me. You expected a raging asshole and so I played the part. I could have called or written, but I chose to stay away."

Tate put his hand on my shoulder and stared at me directly. "Lets both promise to give this brother thing a better try."

A grin tugged at my lips. "Deal."

"This is nice." Caius's white teeth flashed against his dark skin. "We were wondering when the other packs would finally acknowledge how awesome our alpha was."

"Slow your roll, man," Xan cautioned by holding up both hands. "We need to keep our alpha nice and humble. The way we like him."

"You two seriously just need to shut the fuck up sometimes." I laughed feeling lighter than I had ever felt before.

All of Raff's pack seemed to startle at the sound of my laughter, almost in disbelief at hearing it. I guess in front of them I never had a reason to be happy before. Their alpha stepped forward assessing me and my men, and for once he didn't appear to find anything lacking.

"The first change together as a pack and the creation of the pack bonds is a special time. I'm sorry we intruded on it." He reached out his hand.

I accepted the shake. We *might* have both applied more than the necessary amount of pressure during it. Deep down, we are always alphas.

"We should head home." Raff circled his arm around his mate's waist as she put her head on his shoulder.

Tate hesitated looking at both Akela and I before speaking. "I'd like to visit when you get more settled."

"That would be great," Akela replied warmly but

Tate waited for me to respond.

I had to clear my throat before I was able. "I'd like that too."

Tate pulled us into another three-person hug. I would've complained about the possible fractured rib if I hadn't been so damn full of joy at having my brother back in my life. We watched Raff's pack head back to their vehicles and drive away. Something instinctual in us needed to see them leave our pack lands before we went back inside.

"Is something burning?" Xan asked.

"Oh, shit!" Kyle exclaimed. "My brownies!" He ran in.

"I'll go open the windows," Luke said and followed.

Akela held my arm, stopping me from trailing the rest of them inside. I could feel sorrow pulsing down our mate bond as she turned me to face her. "You doubted I'd stay?" Her hand rested on my cheek keeping my eyes angled her way.

"I had to create a hostage situation to get you to be with me. There was a chance you wouldn't choose me." The words burned like acid to admit.

She winced. "Oh, Miles. I was such a fool to not see it earlier. You've always been everything I required. You created exactly what I needed. I felt so much guilt thinking you ditched your brother. Wondering how I could justify telling them I wanted to be with you. I love Tate, and thought you hurt him when you left him with us. But I see now you did it to save him. You even created this entire horrible situation with Chloe so I could go from the role of betrayer to savior. You always act like the bad guy so the rest of us can feel like good guys. But Miles, you are a good man. I see that." She paused and gently kissed my lips. "I love you for that."

My eyes closed as I absorbed those sweet words. I pulled her to me and held her tight. Burying my face in her coconut-scented hair before I confessed it all. "I honestly thought I would never hear you say that to me. Man, I wanted you to so badly, so many times."

Tears glistened in her eyes when she lifted her head to face me. "I'm sorrier than I can say."

I nudged her chin. "None of that now. I knew admitting you loved me was going to be the hardest part. Now, we can move on to the easy things."

Akela laughed as she dashed away a lone tear. "You and I are due for some easy."

"That's the spirit." I slung my arm around her shoulders and headed us back to the house. "We need to find a new place to live as a pack. Luke likes colder climates. Kyle needs to be away from big cities but have the fastest Wi-Fi possible, but Able can't live anywhere he might have a police record on file."

"This is the easy stuff?" my mate sputtered.

"We got this," I said with full bravado. "Oh, and you should find mates for Caius and Xan as soon as possible. Those two are a bunch of man whores, always a slew of jilted lovers creating havoc down at the shop."

"Sure," was her droll reply. "I'll get right on it."

My grin was almost manic as I opened the door for her, my mate, my love. "Perfect! I can't wait to tell them."

The End

ACKNOWLEDGEMENTS

I want to give a special thanks to my dearest beta readers, Kelsey and Lori. You ladies keep me writing with your positive feedback and helpful suggestions. It is no small favor to read the same book over and over! I know. That is why I love you both.

To my editor of the Survival series, Lisa at Evernight Publishing, a special thanks as well. She keeps me looking polished and catches all the blunders my eyes skate right over.

It takes a village to write a good book!

MARIA MERCURIO

EVERNIGHT PUBLISHING ®

www.evernightpublishing.com

www.ingramcontent.com/pod-product-compliance
Lightning Source LLC
Chambersburg PA
CBHW022130170626
46808CB00002B/928